Erich Romberg

Mystical stories in and about Ireland

About the stories in the stories

Vol. 1

Dedication

The Art

Storytelling is an intimate and interactive art. A storyteller tells from memory rather than reading from a book. A tale is not just the spoken equivalent of a literary short story. It has no set text, but is endlessly re-created in the telling. The listener is an essential part of the storytelling process. For stories to live, they need the hearts, minds and ears of listeners. Without the listener there is no story.

www.storytellersofireland.org

Erich Romberg

Mystical stories in and about Ireland

About the stories in the stories

Vol. 1

Where the sky touches the land

Imprint

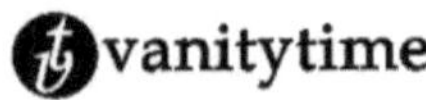 vanitytime

 Printing and distribution on behalf of the author:

tredition GmbH, Heinz-Beusen-Stieg 5, 22926 Ahrensburg, Germany

ISBN

Paperback 978-3-384-12821-8

Hardcover 978-3-384-12822-5

E-Book 978-3-384-12823-2

Email: storyteller@vanitytime.de

Table of contents

Foreword

From 1993, the narrator lived in Kiltimagh, a small town in the west of Ireland, for about 10 years. This is also the period in which the stories in the planned book series are told. This book is the first in the series and is not a narrative about his life in Ireland, even though some episodes are set in real places but generally have a fictional content. You can see this period as a bridge between ancient and modern Ireland. Modern Ireland is not necessarily worse, in many ways even better than the old one. But above all it is different. He got to know Ireland during this transitional period. He had heard a lot about the old Ireland. This old Ireland, characterised by poverty, is more likely to be reflected in Heinrich Böll's 'Irish Diary' from 1957 - from a German perspective - or from an Irish perspective in 'Angela's Ashes' by the Irish-American author Frank McCourt from 1996. At the time, the country was already a member of the EU and on its way to becoming the economic miracle country of the 1990s. The term 'Celtic Tiger' was coined and the idea of unlimited growth developed in people's minds. The first setback came with the crash of the Telekom share price in 2001, when many people sold their houses, land and property, which they had been selling like sour beer for years at dumping prices. A previously unknown construction boom caused the value of their property to explode and flushed money into the coffers of the formerly poor. Many sensed enormous potential returns in the purchase of telecoms shares. They sold their land for less than it was worth in order to cash in on their good fortune. Many fell back into the poverty from which they had come. Only now they no longer owned land. Families and friendships broke up. He had experienced this personally. So he is far from romanticising this country. With the global economic and financial crisis in 2008, the experience of finiteness finally returned. He was no longer living in Ireland at the time, but of course he visited his old hometown of Kiltimagh from time to time. The dream of prosperity is over for many.

He mixes reality and fiction in his stories. He is interested in traditional storytelling from ancient times in this remarkable country. The stories he writes down here were written during his time in Ireland, among other places. Originally, he had no intention of publishing them. It was the sheer joy of storytelling that led him to write them down. The idea came about at a storytelling festival in his home town of Kiltimagh, which took place once a year. The time of storytellers was actually over, television had long since taken over the function of entertainment and smartphones had yet to be invented. But once a year, this tradition was revived. The storytellers travelled from place to place to present their art and demonstrate their skills. The storyteller regrets a little that he didn't get to experience the storytelling tradition. But he has heard a lot from Irish friends who grew up with this tradition. Especially on long winter evenings, people would meet in the pubs to listen to the storytellers, who could be found in almost every village. It was not unusual for the stories to go on for several evenings. Many could hardly wait for the next evening to listen to the continuation of a story from the previous evening by the crackling peat fire. The storytellers were the mediums of the past. The stories often began with "In my grandfather's day...". It was not uncommon for the stories to reach far back into the past and deal with events that had supposedly taken place generations ago. True and mysterious alternated. The true stories almost always had a secret. Nowhere else did he experience the belief in the supernatural as vividly as in Ireland. In conversations with friends, he often heard about ghostly apparitions that were told with such seriousness that it was hard to doubt the truth of the experiences. Even though he often suspected he was being taken for a ride when he heard less serious stories, he is now convinced that people in Ireland really aren't joking about such things. Perhaps this can be gauged from the fact that the inclusion of elfin areas was part of Irish road and building planning. People behaved in such a way as not to antagonise the elves. They were taken into consideration in Ireland, and even if you wanted to build in Ireland as a non-Irish person, it was advisable to do so. Belief in the supernatural was deeply rooted in Ireland. So it was only natural that it was also reflected in the stories of the Irish. So when telling stories in or about Ireland, they should contain a more or less large portion of mysticism alongside the everyday. It is best to be infected by the magic of the stories told in Ireland. Not everything in life can be grasped with logic, just as events cannot always be clearly explained in retrospect with so-called "common sense". An Irish story is best when it has both the natural and the mystical. It is then up to the reader to decide which interpretation to allow. The storyteller himself is far more captivated by mystical interpretations of stories than by the banal reality that we have enough of in everyday life.

In his Irish days, there were still two pubs in his small town where this tradition of storytelling was cultivated - at least occasionally. The stories of the storyteller himself sometimes took place in these pubs. He particularly remembers Joyce's Bar, where flickering peat fires were a constant source of storytelling. The unforgettable old country lady Anne Joe has a firm place in the narrator's memory; she is the protagonist in the stories several times. When she died, he was still able to say goodbye to her. She died with her typical smile and the words:

"I'm going home now."

About three years ago, someone remembered Joyce's Bar something like this:

"JOYCE'S was our "fairy fortress", there was always magic in the air, from dusk till dawn, soul food ... long stories and fairy tales, my vision of heaven...". There is no better way to put it.

The stories begin with a poem about Kiltimagh. This is where he learnt storytelling. He tries to convey to the reader the atmosphere of sitting round a crackling peat fire with friends and someone telling one of those stories that Ireland has produced in such great numbers.

The first story in this volume takes place in one of his two favourite pubs, Lil's Bar, by a crackling peat fire. Where else? As the only guest at this time of day, the narrator is allowed to write a story at the regulars' table. The title story is born. It is about a strange encounter with an old man who expresses an equally strange wish. The attentive reader will not fail to notice that the narrator encounters himself.

By the time he has finished the story, the pub has filled up with guests and the regulars invite him to stay at the pub to tell the story he has written down. Afterwards, the men at the regulars' table discuss the story and quickly guess its meaning. As they liked the story, they ask the storyteller if he can tell more stories. He tells the second story about a strange firebird that carries the entire consciousness of the world at the beginning of time.

The idea for the next story was born in Joyce's Bar, on one of the days of a storytelling festival, the storyteller's first in this country. The story of Saóirse and Méabh also begins on a weekend during a storytelling competition. It tells the story of the nomad girl Saóirse, who has just turned sixteen. On the first day of the festival, she is allowed to gain unaccompanied experience in the small town of Kiltimagh for the first time. It is a time full of stories and Saóirse learns about love. Watching over all of this is the wise old Méabh, who advises the girl to listen only to her heart. This is not so easy and as a result she ends up making a difficult and painful decision

The narrator speaks from the perspective of Saóirse, who is equipped by Méabh in such a way that she is not recognised as a nomad girl.

In Ireland, the nomads are called Tinkers or Travellers, the travelling people. The nomads themselves prefer the term Traveller and call themselves Pavee. The Pavee are ethnically Irish themselves and have historically been excluded from the majority population through socio-economic processes. In the days before modern media, they played an important role in the dissemination of news, stories and music. Irish folk can also largely be traced back to them. Without them, Irish culture would not be what it is today.

The Pavee lived in large family groups, mostly in wagon camps. Irish society was deeply prejudiced against this part of their people. The short episode in a shop from Saóirse's point of view at the beginning of the story was also experienced by the narrator, except that he was on the other side, in this shop.

Old Méabh is the big mum in her family and was also highly respected by the other Pavee families. She was an absolute role model, and not just for Saóirse. She is known as the 'old Méabh', whereby 'old' refers less to her years and more to her wisdom. Her authority is not based on strictness, but on her kind wisdom.

In the fourth story, an overtired driver is travelling west towards Galway along the sometimes narrow roads. As he is about to fall asleep, he leaves the road to rest. In the darkness, someone knocks on the rear window and asks for a lift in accent-free German. During the journey, he recognises a former best friend from his youth in the person who got on the train, and a journey back in time to a repressed past begins.

Finally, the fifth and last story is about a storyteller who has forgotten how to tell stories.

He spends a night in the former Joyce's and suddenly finds himself forced into the role of an executioner. As if by magic, he regains his storytelling ability. Let's wait and see how much mysticism and magic there really is.

Sleeping small town (poetry)

Asleep you lie

Small town,

as in grey times.

Your heroes

have never died,

they have not been born

for a long time.

The courage of your ancestors

lies in their immutability.

Even the movements stand

frozen in the streets.

The shock wave of time

has rolled over you,

the third millennium

takes place elsewhere.

Only the time traveller

sees the deep sleep recede,

the swaying of the dream raft

in the storm of thunderstorm of times.

Altruistic Time Hexagram (Figures Poetry)

time

to stay for a while

but to leave the stage in time.

Time is life, love, laughter and suffering.

Flowing life, emerging, is passing away,

passing and fading until the end of time.

eternal reborn, sunlight flooded through,

the infinity laughs about the lust for life.

Live, love, laugh and suffer

to linger in

time.

A look into the future

It was a rainy Sunday morning and I was sitting in Lil's Bar. Apart from Vera, Tom and me, there was no one else here. Vera looked to be in her mid-seventies, her brother maybe a year older, I had never asked her. As if I'd had a premonition, I had my writing utensils with me. I ordered a pint of Guinness and told Vera that I wanted to write a story. Stories characterise this country and the people here love to hear and tell stories. They laugh at the funny ones, get serious about the thoughtful ones and get creeped out by the scary ones. Storytelling is a serious matter that is fun. So it was only logical that Vera started the ceremony straight away and lit a peat fire in the fireplace. Indeed, the flickering and crackling fire created an atmosphere that stimulated my writing. I was allowed to take the seat by the fire, which was actually reserved for special guests and remained empty in their absence. So it was an honour to be allowed to sit here. There was only one condition: The regulars would arrive in about two hours, then I would have to take another table. Tom was actually one of them, but he preferred to sit at or behind the bar when the others weren't there. He just nodded in agreement when Vera put the beer on the sacred table. So my story couldn't be too long, because I expected to have to tell it. As I was writing it in German, I made a few notes in English in the margin. In addition to a German-English dictionary, I always had an English-Irish dictionary with me because I used Irish terms from time to time - smartphones didn't exist back then. I didn't realise then that the Irish dictionary would become so important for this story.

I never knew what I would write when I sat down. So I started with a walk from Cultrasna, the neighbourhood I lived in at the time, down the often-travelled path to the River Glore, with my dog of course. For something to happen, I had to meet someone. As the story progressed, I realised that I had to find a suitable name for my encounter from the dictionary.

Where the sky touches the land

The night is clear and cold. Silence has fallen over the land, broken only by Leo's familiar panting. He seeks me out and sometimes I can feel his body against my leg. The stars of the universe fulfil a very private task today; I know that they are only shining up there for Leo and me. Houses and huts are scattered around, painted into the landscape by an aesthetic god. With my gaze still fixed on the light of infinity, my steps carry me onwards. At night, the path down to the Glore River makes me realise and forget a thousand things; that's why I love these late walks.

Suddenly there is an old, shrivelled little man. Encounters at such a late hour are rare here.

"I was expecting you, how are you? " he speaks to me. A strange greeting; I don't know him.

"Not bad," I reply, surprised, and try to remember, in case there's anything to remember.

"It's already late, the river down there is waiting for us," he continues.

"The Glore?" I ask unnecessarily. The little man pauses for a while, then says:

"Yes, yes, my river, our river."

I caught myself and say that I don't remember him.

"I am who I am - Támé tú Féin."

Strange words and a strange name, I know I've never heard it before. I ask him where he lives.

"Where the sky touches the land," the old man says more to himself than to me.

He seems to love being vague and points his bony finger at Leo:

"That's a nice dog."

As if Leo had understood him, he cuddles up to him. He seems to like the old man, because this trusting behaviour towards strangers is unusual for him. The old man pats his head. We talk about my dog, about the weather in this neighbourhood and about this beautiful night. Then the old man's eyes flash at me with a fire that seems to surpass even the glow of the stars.

"We meet because we have overcome the time between us for a little while," he says mysteriously, "we have to use it by doing me a little favour that will also benefit you."

This mysterious puzzle game is starting to appeal to me, or is it not a game at all? I ask cautiously whether I would be able to.

"Certainly, in terms of the effort involved, it's really only a small thing, hardly worth mentioning. But it's very important."

It feels strange and I say:

"Small effort and great significance, what is it?"

"Because of the importance of the moment, I don't want to tell you until just beforehand. But I can tell you this much: it's a good thing. The moment you do it, you will realise the significance and be free afterwards."

"If it's good, then so be it."

"Great," says the old man, "let's go down to the Glore."

He grabs my wrist and pulls me with him. As I walk beside him, he lets go again. His gait is determined, his arms swing briskly against his body. His steps are as silent as those of a shadow. The silence is again broken only by Leo's pitter-patter and his panting, thoughts racing through my head. I furtively observe the scaly shadow next to me, nothing about him indicates what he might expect from me. Then we hear the familiar roar of the Glore, which flows through the valley at considerable speed. Leo's panting is now swallowed up by the sound of the river and a little later we are standing on the narrow bridge. The old man has hurried ahead of me, reached the other bank and swings over the waist-high quarry stone wall onto the field beyond with an ease I wouldn't have believed him capable of. Leo follows him wagging his tail, he loves this place. I follow him and we walk for a while in the direction of the river in the field, the old man always three steps ahead. Now he jumps over a low ledge and stops after a few steps. The old man has turned his face to the west and stares silently into the current. He stands there as if rooted to the spot, a gnarled little tree. I have reached him, but I don't dare speak to him. After he hasn't moved for a while, I sit down on the embankment, close my eyes and let the melody of the flow take effect on me. A sense of peace and freedom fills me, and neither the old man nor Leo disturb me. I almost believe that he is listening to the quiet legends of this clear night, the intoxicating music of the river, and that the synergetic experience of shared enjoyment is the favour. When I wake up after a long time from a kind of trance, the old man is sitting next to me and looking at me.

"This is where the sky touches the land," he says in a low whisper. After a while, he asks in the same whisper:

"Are you willing to do me the favour now, then I will reveal it?"

"What should I do?" I breathe, the night not allowing a loud word.

"Follow me into the water and cleanse me, as you know from the Bible."

His strange request takes my breath away, but I can see from his face that he's not joking.

"I don't expect you to understand yet," he knows my astonishment, "it's not a big deal for you today, but it means a lot to us."

He walks the few steps to the bank and without another word the strange old man steps into the river and kneels in the middle of the current, the water just reaching his hips. I don't bother to get rid of my clothes. Silently, obedient as a lamb, I follow him. The cool water washes around my knees, the current tugs at my legs. When I reach the person being baptised, he has folded his hands and bowed his head. He says solemnly: "Tá mé tú féin, only time unites us."

After these enigmatic words, I pause next to him for a moment. Déjà vu! I realise what I have to do and I understand what I am doing. I grab the back of his neck and gently pull him backwards, he willingly dives under. After a few seconds, I slide my other hand into the water under his head and lift his upper body out. Without hesitation, the old man rises and says in a still muffled voice:

"Thank you, my boy. Our destiny has been fulfilled, we are free. Mistakes and folly will accompany our path, and over the years we will learn to separate the wheat from the chaff. You have freed me from my folly tonight and I can return to my origins, God bless you."

He steps out of the water and, without turning round again, walks down the riverbank. I have grasped the sacredness of the moment, remain lost in thought and watch the old man's rejuvenating figure. Soon her outline disappears where the sky touches the land.

A look at the times

In the meantime, the men from the regulars' table had arrived and Vera briefly explained why I was allowed to sit there. I had finished my story and put my utensils away to sit at another table.

"Not so fast!" said one of the new arrivals, whom I had seen here several times before, but I had never spoken to him before.

"If you've written a story at our table, we want to hear it too. Our table has magical powers of inspiration and we would like to hear how well it works! Stay with us, the table is big enough."

So I was invited to stay on. As I reported above, I was prepared to have to tell the story here. At first I pretended to be coy, but this fuelled them all the more, which of course I was prepared for. I finally gave in and apologised as a precaution for a possibly poor translation, as I had written the story in German. I didn't mention the marginal notes in English, as the inaccuracies in the translation would certainly be numerous enough as it was.

"You'll be fine," said the speaker, "after all, you're at our inspirational table, it will help you."

To prevent my throat from drying out, the speaker first ordered a pint of ale.

I placed both hands on this table and said aloud that he may pour inspiration over me.

"Dear table, pour your inspiration over me."

The men laughed and said that nothing could happen now. In the meantime, many new guests had come into the pub and Tom called out to them that I was going to tell them a story that nobody knew yet. Some of them immediately approached our table with their glasses of beer in one hand to hear my story. There was no turning back now, so I told the story, which the reader already knew, as best I could in English.

"Where the sky touches the land.... "

When I finished, there was sincere applause from everyone who had listened, at least nobody made a funny remark.

"Very good, really good," said the men at the table. Although we didn't live in a Gaeltacht region here, their Irish was enough to understand the few terms I used. They actually discussed my story and quickly understood what I was trying to say. I would have thought it would be harder to interpret, but I was in a round that had won most of the quiz competitions here in the village that were held on some weekends. I'll have to think of something more difficult next time. Now it was my turn to offer compliments, but the speaker from before said dryly:

"You sit at the table of wisdom, you can expect that." A cheerful laugh broke out and I had to laugh too; yes, that's how they are.

"I'm sure you have more stories," said Tom.

In fact, I had a bunch of handwritten manuscripts with me, but I hadn't translated them at that point. I thought about what would fit now, and the Firebird came to mind. After looking into my future, a look back in time would be a suitable continuation. But this story contains many terms whose English meaning I didn't know. I asked for some time to look them up in the dictionary. After a quarter of an hour I was done, but despite the dictionary I still had problems finding the right translation for some terms. I apologised in advance if one or two things didn't come across quite as I had imagined. Tom suggested that another pint might make my story flow better and a pint of beer was on the house. In fact, after a few draughts from the glass, I took a relatively relaxed approach. So I began with the words:

"After giving you a glimpse into my future in my last story, as you so aptly discovered, I am now broadening the horizon and opening the window for you to take a look into the future. So listen to the story of the firebird!" At this point there was advance applause, in which everyone in the pub joined in. I heard the shouts: Open the window. The atmosphere couldn't have been better. Then I began to tell the story:

The Firebird

In the beginning of time, a great beautiful bird rose from the maw of the mighty volcano on the eastern circles of the earth, along with glowing stone and ash, long before the ancestor of our species left the water.

The egg of the firebird had incubated for myriads of years at the bottom of the volcano, only to break its diamond shell in the seething embers of the fire on the very first day of earth's existence. Like the protective shell of the egg, the bird's plumage was made of the finest diamond and the fire of its dress glittered far across the land.

The firebird rose thousands of miles above the glowing maw, carrying the consciousness of the world within it.

After reaching the outermost circle of the earth in steep flight over days, weeks and moons, it feared to leave the protective power of the earth and swivelled into an orbit on which it circled it from then on. It flew around the earth countless times, while many millions of years passed.

As the bird carried all consciousness within itself, time did not pass in vain. He thought about the meaning of his being and came to the conclusion that all this fire of the earth must be part of a great whole, created to bring forth him, the firebird. In the beginning was the egg, he thought, and this thought manifested itself in him. In the flow of time, he recognised a meaning behind all this being. Long before he was born, these fires must have been burning and the blazing embers were not an end in themselves. All this flickering and burning led to one goal: to give birth to him and make him the bearer of consciousness.

There were many fires in the universe, more numerous and more powerful than any on earth, and once upon a time they were a great whole. Long after their creation, they separated so that at least one of them could fulfil the purpose of its burning and produce a diamond egg.

After circling the earth for myriads of years, the radiant bird realised the deeper meaning of its existence.

He had reached the limits of his own thinking. Although he believed that all his consciousness was the cause of existence, he could not find the meaning of his existence in the next few myriads of years. He sensed that he alone would not fulfil the meaning. Therefore, he decided to return to complete his task.

From the deep expanses of space, it plummeted to earth, which in the meantime had formed a dense atmosphere. It surrounded it like a viscous pulp and when it plunged into it so abruptly, the diamond plumage heated up; the bird glowed and burst into blazing fire. When its body reached the ground, it was burnt to ashes.

And lo and behold, out of the ashes rose the phoenix, more beautiful and wiser than the old firebird; but it no longer carried all the consciousness. He had freed himself from the limits of knowledge and flew higher than his father ever had.

A large part of the consciousness remained on earth. The ashes mixed in the swamps and after a few billion years a lizard crawled ashore, carrying the sleeping consciousness within it. It was a very long time before it awoke and realised that it was the cause of existence.

Over time, consciousness has spread over many billions of parts, constantly renewing itself, like the phoenix, to become more beautiful and wiser than the old.

Since that time, countless eyes have gazed at the stars in the night and most of them do not realise that they are looking at themselves. The bearers of these eyes commit and desire foolish things and believe they are living for them. But the old firebird knew about all this and that is why he had distributed consciousness so lavishly.

One of thousands of pairs of eyes in every generation search the night for the phoenix that carries the consciousness of this world with them. The time will come when it will glow again and the consciousness of the world will reunite. A new phoenix will be born from the ashes: Bigger, more powerful and more beautiful. It will once again carry the meaning of existence and its spawn will be knowledge, long after the foolish things of this world have burnt out.

In the beginning was the egg, and at the end is the realisation."

The pub had filled up considerably in the meantime and there was absolute silence while I talked. Many people had crowded round our table to be able to hear better. Now the tension turned into applause and some of those present patted me on the back. I have to admit that I enjoyed it and also felt that I had managed it reasonably well. Sure, I was able to do it more accurately in the later translation in the quiet room, but you can read about that elsewhere.

As expected, the men at the table began to think about and discuss the story, and Vera also joined in. I won't go into the details of the discussion here, because then I would deprive the reader of the pleasure of thinking for themselves about what the narrator wanted to say with this story.

Just so much, Tom opened the discussion:

"Spontaneously, I would say it's a parable about people."

I say to the reader, it's not wrong, but it's more.

From the ashes (Poetry)

The phoenix rises from the ashes,
having once been human.
He is perfect,
does not accuse,
does not lecture.
 Creation is right,
Good and evil,
greedy and modest,
holy and voluptuous;
ying and yang.
He no longer improves
this created world,
it is as it is,
right and wrong.
He no longer teaches
God and the devil.
They created
man and phoenix
from water and fire.

Time dilemma (Poetry)

The boat glides in the vortex of time,
escape from the turbulent fluctuations of forgotten
existence.
The future appears in the circle of the horizon,
where the dream lake plunges into infinity.
The driftwood meanders in the storm of time,
from present to present without a will,
loses itself in being as it was.
There is no way out of the void,
not a sphere of life that leads to the future.
Life is in the drive and lust is in the drive.
Memories are the will-o'-the-wisps of time,
that flow back into life and drown.
The future, however unattainable it may seem on
the horizon,
is the vital source of life.
To where the lake of dreams pours into the sky,
the creature lays its sinew.
But it does not fulfil itself in the fluctuating time,
that does not lead out of the now.
Only when time freezes does existence plunge into
the abyss,
which is called the future.

The Nomad Girl and the Old Méabh

Saóirse and Méabh

Nobody knows how old Méabh really is. The elders of the clan say she was old and wise when they were children themselves. Some say behind closed doors that she is "the Méabh", the former warrior queen of Connacht from the old Irish legends. The old Méabh is no longer warlike - if she ever was. She is wise, humorous and infinitely patient, even if she can be merciless in her judgement when someone goes over the top.

Saóirse loves being with her, because the old Méabh knows many exciting stories from a time when Ireland was very different from today. She is a healer, fortune teller, counsellor and final authority in disputes, but also when two young people say yes to each other. The members listen to her advice and have done well with it for decades. Seemingly irreconcilable quarrellers have given in to many a wise saying, first grumbling, then realising that it was a good thing.

At almost sixteen years old, Saóirse hasn't travelled much and has only seen Galway and Castlebar. The old Méabh has seen the world in her younger years - if she was ever young. She is even said to have been to Dublin, when Dublin was still called Baile Átha Cliath.

Saóirse and her clan are among the last nomads in Ireland, and in recent decades many of them have settled down. Their caravan is now pulled by an old Opel, and because petrol has become expensive, they can no longer drive around as much. Saóirse no longer remembers the days when horses pulled the carts and there was still food for them even when times were hard for the people. Sometimes she wishes those times were back because she loves horses so much. She is also tired of travelling to the same places over and over again. How nice it was back then when you didn't know in the morning where you would set up camp in the evening. The people were also much nicer back then. Méabh sometimes says that the villagers gave them food and drink when they arrived somewhere. In return, they received stories, music and news, which did not spread everywhere back then, when there was no modern media. The people were poor, but what they had, they shared. Saóirse loves to hear the stories about the festivals that were celebrated with the villagers.

How different it is today!

The villages have become towns and the people are rich. But the rich don't like to share, and today the Travellers have to compete with those who have remained poor.

In the past, people were happy if someone repaired their kettles and pots or sharpened their knives and scissors for a few pennies.

Today, only a few knives and scissors are sharpened, and pots are bought new if they have a dent or are leaking. You can buy them for I£4 in the Dune Stores. There is not much left for the nomads to do today. Social welfare is not enough to buy petrol. If Méabh didn't occasionally earn some extra money by reading cards or palmistry, sometimes they wouldn't be able to leave Castlebar at all. Saóirse remembers an episode in a small town. When she was walking through the streets with her brothers, people behaved very strangely, as if they were afraid. They rushed from the street into their houses. Saóirse wanted to buy something sweet in a small shop, but the owner had locked the shop, although Saóirse could see through the shop windows that there were children inside. When one of her brothers knocked on the door, a man in a white coat gestured that the shop was closed. When Saóirse later asked the old Méabh, she said:

"There are families who are so poor that they beg in the villages and towns. But the settled ones accumulate money and other goods. You could say that their possessions also become immobile, even their money. They don't like it when the state of their lives and possessions changes.

If a sedentary person has a certain amount of money, it is worrying for them if this decreases. That would mean that their money is wandering. But they hate it when people or things move. That's why they try to hold on to everything they own. There are people among them who already have the breath of death written all over their faces and who have more money than they could ever spend in the last days of their lives. Nevertheless, they cling to every penny of their possessions. They even try to scrape together even more. When death finally overtakes these people, they are terrified of it, they weep and wail because they know that it will take everything they own.

When one of us comes to them, they are afraid of having to give up some of their possessions. Whether we ask them or not, the mere sight of us frightens them. They say we Tinkers are beggars and thieves. They don't distinguish between begging and stealing, and from their point of view that is understandable, because both mean a reduction in their possessions; that is why they fear us like death. These people are poorer than a starving beggar, so we should pray for them. Yes, the old Méabh is very wise and knows a lot about everything in this world.

Saóirse is determined never to ask a sedentary person for anything, because she doesn't want anyone to be afraid of her.

Then her sixteenth birthday arrives and the old Méabh calls her in. The old woman's wise eyes scan her from head to toe.

"You have become a young girl, and it has not escaped my notice that, without your realising it, young lads have cast an interested eye on you from time to time. You have been protected by your family so far, I know that your mind is honest and your character firm. You know little more about the people of this world than I have told you. That is why I have decided with your parents that you may spend Saturdays and Sundays in Kiltimagh for a whole month. You will be dropped off at the church in the village around midday and your father will pick you up again at midnight. I have saved up for you and you will receive forty pounds for each weekend so that you are independent and can enjoy your free time. Use the time to learn as much as you can about the people."

Saóirse feels a joyful leap in her heart; she has long secretly wished to be able to spend time in a town or village without the supervision of her brothers.

"The day after tomorrow," the old woman continued, "you come to me in the morning, because it's your first Saturday. I will give you clothes that are no different from those in the village, otherwise the people there would recognise the Pavee. Remember what I once told you about the sedentary people and their fears, but look at them without prejudice."

Saóirse eagerly awaits the day. Many expectations in her head paint pictures in her impatient soul. She resolves to learn a lot about people. One day she wants to be as wise as the old Méabh. Whatever the upright posture and firm character mean, she will find out and preserve it.

It is Saturday. Saóirse has slept fitfully during the night. At nine in the morning, she knocks on Méabh's door. When the old woman's face appears in the crack of the door, a broad smile flits across her wrinkled face.

"I've been expecting you," she says and invites the girl in. On the table are jeans, a white blouse, a sleeveless overcoat and a black coat with fluffy faux fur. On the floor between the chair legs are mid-height leather shoes. Saóirse can hardly believe that these are supposed to be for her. A little later, she marvels at herself in the old-fashioned dresser mirror. She can hardly believe that she is the girl in the mirror. Then the old woman points to the sofa and Saóirse sits down unsteadily on the front edge of the cushion. Old Méabh sits down next to her and takes her hand.

"I don't want to give you any long explanations or confuse you with rules of behaviour, just some advice if you want it."

The girl's open eyes gaze into the depths of the wise old woman.

"Yes," breathes the little girl, "anything you're willing to give me."

The old Méabh gives a satisfied grunt and begins to fix her eyes firmly on the girl:

"In everything you intend to do, there is only one authority, and that is your heart. Before you decide to do this or that, go inside yourself and ask yourself if it feels right. Forget everything you've heard about right and wrong, don't follow rigid morals. Don't ask your mind or your desires whether what you want to do is right or wrong, just listen to your heart, that's all I need to tell you."

Saóirse looks at the old woman with wide eyes; from her parents she is used to there being a rule for everything that you have to follow. She has never managed to stick to all these rules. But the advice the old woman gives her sounds so simple. As if she has guessed the girl's thoughts, she says:

"Oh, my darling, it's not as easy as it sounds. The heart speaks softly and is often drowned out by thoughts or desires. And yet it's the only thing you should listen to when it matters. If you follow this advice, I won't worry about you.

Saóirse does not want old Méabh to worry about her, and she is determined to listen to her heart, however quietly he may be. The old woman nods again, as if she has guessed the little girl's thoughts, and says:

"I don't have to worry about you".

Alone in the city

Around midday, her father drops her off at the church.

He would be back here in about twelve hours to take her home. May God protect her. Saóirse sees tears in her father's eyes and tells him not to worry about her, that her heart will protect her. The father smiles at these words. "Of course."

Then she is finally alone for the first time in her young life. She strolls slowly towards the city centre. The first pub appears on her left; she knows there are seventeen of them here. An old lady with alert eyes stands in the doorway and looks at her impassively.

"Hello, hello," says Saóirse, a little embarrassed. "I've never seen you here before."

"I'm visiting, I have to leave again tonight."

"Welcome, God bless you."

Saóirse feels a joyful leap in her heart; it is the first conversation she has had alone outside her clan. She now walks on towards the city centre with much more confidence. There are lots of people on the street. It is very different from when people looked at her and her brothers with suspicious glances. Apart from the glances of a few young lads, nobody seems to be interested in her. That's fine by her, because the looks from the boys alone are embarrassing. She stops at a burger joint and remembers that she has a lot of money in her pocket, more than she needs to afford a cheeseburger. Less out of hunger - she has eaten at home - she decides to buy a cheeseburger. A young man is standing behind the counter in the snack bar. It's busy and it takes her ten minutes to get to the other side of the counter.

"And what do you fancy?" he asks with a suggestive smile. She stares wide-eyed into his beautiful but somewhat cheeky eyes. Her face gets hot, she's obviously overconfident.

What am I doing here," it flashed through her mind. Her heart didn't want this cheeseburger, but she had an unknown feeling in her heart, it wasn't the cheeseburger. She looks at the vendor and lowers her eyes in embarrassment.

"Sorry," Saóirse stammers, "I... I... don't know."
She becomes embarrassed. She feels her face
getting hotter and doesn't dare look at the man
behind the counter again. Then she just wants to get
out.

"Sorry," she says again and leaves the counter in a
hurry. She can still hear the shop assistant asking
her to wait a moment, then she reaches the door of
the snack bar to save herself. As if she were being
chased, she runs down the street and only comes to
a halt when the crowd gets smaller and she is
standing next to a kind of adventure park for
children. She peers into the park through the
boundary beams and watches the little ones letting
off steam on the equipment. She feels a jumble of
emotions rising up inside her. In this confusion, she
keeps thinking that she has to listen to her heart.
But no matter how hard she tries, her heart remains
silent.

The children in the park whoop with delight and for
a moment the volcano inside her calms down. Then
her head starts to work.

'You're stupid,' he says, 'it's so beautiful in the city
and you're standing here being a coward. It can't be
that bad. Nothing has happened. '

With a jolt, she turns away from the children's park and heads back to the centre. The crowds have thickened and outside a pub she sees a group of boys fooling around with a couple of girls. She tries to walk past them when a boy speaks to her.

"Hello, pretty girl, where are you going? It's a party here!"

Suddenly he stands in front of her and looks her cheekily in the eye. A girl from the group says:

"Leave the girl alone, Kevin."

Saóirse is confused and doesn't know what to do.

"What party?" she asks, more out of embarrassment than interest.

"Ah..., well, the party."

Now the boy seems a little embarrassed. A girl detaches herself from the group and hooks her arm, she is about their age.

"Don't listen to him," she says scornfully, "he's a bit daft."

Although Saóirse doesn't know this girl, it does her good that she takes care of her.

"I'm Máire, I take it you're a stranger here? I've never seen you before.

"Yes, I have to leave again at midnight."

"Then we still have enough time to get to know each other."

"Cinderella!" shouts one of the boys, amused.

"Shut up, you're just stupid country boys."

Turning to Saóirse, she says:

"Do you want to hear the storytellers here in this pub?"

"Storyteller?" asks Saóirse, confused.

"Isn't that why you're here?"

"No, I'm in the village alone for the first time to get to know the people."

Máire looks at Saóirse in amazement.

"Are you saying you've never been anywhere alone?"

"Yes," replies Saóirse, "I only turned sixteen two days ago."

"So what? I was here alone in the village when I was eight or even earlier."

Saóirse looks at her with wide eyes, alone with eight would not be possible in her clan. But then Máire says.

"Don't worry, we'll manage. First of all, come with us here to the pub and listen to the storytellers' stories. You probably don't even know that the storytellers' festival starts this weekend. Anyone here who wants to is invited to tell a story."

Then she puts her lips to Saóirse's ear and whispers.

"Hardly anyone here tells stories anymore, but we all look forward to the professionals who come to the village every year for the festival and tell old stories, you shouldn't miss it. Today and tomorrow, the country's most famous storytellers are coming to our town to tell stories that will make you laugh or make your blood run cold. Laughter and horror go hand in hand."

"I love exciting stories," says Saóirse happily, "I really enjoy coming along."

"Come on then," says Máire, pulling Saóirse towards the door of the pub, "a very famous storyteller is coming in ten minutes."

"Leave the princess with us," calls an exuberant boy's voice.

"Shut up," shouts Máire scornfully, "get drunk or fuck off home."

Saóirse is impressed by Máire's courage, because she would never have dared to say something like that herself.

Saóirse is in a pub for the first time in her life.

Joyce's is a small room with two counters. On the right, it looks like an old shop. The shelves are lined with tins of beans, packets of cornflakes and other old-fashioned-looking food packaging that you don't find in modern supermarkets. On the right behind the long counter is a friendly-looking old lady pouring beer into a pint glass. A man with long dark hair sits on a stool behind the counter, rolling a cigarette. In front of the bar are men aged between eighteen and eighty and a few groups of younger women. Women sit together on the few benches and talk about the village gossip. There is a babble of voices and laughter from all corners, and Saóirse is happy to see everyone so cheerful.

Máire takes Saóirse by the hand and pulls her to the counter.

"This is Saóirse, Ann," she says to the old lady behind the counter, "she's going out alone for the first time."

She turns to Saóirse and gestures towards the old lady:

"This is Anny Joe, the country lady."

Anny Joe looks at Saóirse with sparkling eyes, her mouth showing a warm girlish smile.

"Welcome to Kiltimagh," she says, "you've picked the best day to visit, one of Ireland's most famous storytellers is about to speak, Pádraig ó Flaherty from Donegal.

Máire orders two 7Up and introduces Saóirse to Paul, Anny Joe's long-haired nephew, who is thoughtfully lighting up a roll-up.

"Hello Saóirse," he says in slow motion as he fills his lungs with smoke, "welcome here," and blows the smoke into the air with relish.

"Hello Paul," Saóirse replies in a friendly manner, "nice to meet you."

Paul nods and something like a smile flits across his face. He looks happy at this moment and inhales again vigorously to increase his well-being.

"Pádraig is brilliant, he will inspire you."

Paul's words sound like millennia-old wisdom, coming slowly and firmly from his mouth in a bass tone. They have managed to make Saóirse burst with curiosity.

A young man with glassy eyes, sitting on the bench at the far end of the bar, jumps up faster than is good for his condition. Staggering, he shows the two girls to their seats, Máire doesn't need to be asked twice and pulls Saóirse towards her.

"Thanks, Joe," she says flippantly and turns to Saóirse: "Box seat."

Joe stares at Saóirse and tries to put on a charming smile, which seems to be difficult for him, because it almost knocks him off his feet.

"Joe's a nice guy," she whispers in Saóirse's ear, "but unfortunately he's usually drunk."
The front door opens and a man of about sixty in a colourful jacket and a wide-brimmed hat comes in. Máire pokes Saóirse in the ribs and whispers excitedly:

"That's him."

The chaos in the pub settles, laughter and chatter dies down and suddenly applause fills the room. Saóirse's eyes are filled with tears, she finds the atmosphere so uplifting. From somewhere in the depths of the room, a raised stool is conjured up and placed in the centre. Nanoseconds later, he sits majestically on it, holding a well-filled pint glass of Guinness in his hand.

Then he begins:

"I'm glad I'm sitting here safe and sound in front of you, enjoying my pint, and," he looks around and, logically, Paul stands next to him and hands him one of his steaming home-rolls. He takes a deep puff and continues, "a good smoke."

He takes a well-measured pause, nods sagely to the others and inhales deeply once more. Somewhere in the room, a fallen hair rumbles to the floor as he finally breaks the silence.

Story about Pádraig's fight with the devil

If I hadn't experienced it for myself, I wouldn't believe it myself.

You know I'm from Glenn Colmcille, and on festival days I get up at half past four in the morning to catch the bus from Donegal Town to Castlebar at about nine o'clock. At this time of year, the sun is already rising in the east as I walk along the lonely roads at half past five. I've never met anyone on my way at this time before. So I was amazed when he suddenly stood in front of me in full life size.

"Hello Pádraig," he said, "are you still crazy enough to think that people are interested in your stories? You should have stayed in bed until the glorious day shines into your room. You're still looking for your old home, you should realise that it no longer exists. You're a fossil who denies progress, nobody wants to hear your hackneyed stories. Today the stories are told on television, professional and crazy, you're an old fool, Pádraig.

Believe me, these words hit me hard and I felt miserable. He was so right. I myself go to one of our pubs several times a week and often the landlord barely notices when I enter. All eyes are on a horse race, hurling or one of the many soaps. In the afternoon, the eyes of the few guests are fixed on the screen. It's not unusual for my friends to not even notice me. As I had nothing to counter this, I asked him:

"Who are you?"

At dawn, I saw a broad grin flit across his face.

"I am your part of what is commonly called the devil."

You can't imagine how terrible fear can be. The blood froze in my veins and an icy chill gripped my body.

"Jesus Christ," I cried, "take Satan away from me."

The devil grinned broadly:

"It's not that simple, it only works like that in bad horror films, I'm a part of you that you can't exorcise."

My mind began to work feverishly. This is a hallucination," I said to myself. I closed my eyes and thought:

'You really can't stand getting up so early.

I was already regretting that I hadn't arrived a day earlier, at a tolerable time for an Irishman.

Then I opened my eyes again, but the monster was still grinning cheekily in my face.

"I told you that you wouldn't get rid of me that easily."

I had to accept it, whether I wanted to or not. The devil was standing before me in the flesh and I, a good Christian, had to come to terms with him. But then Satan's face lost its humiliating grin. I heard his voice almost softly.

"Don't be a fool, don't waste your talent on these useless people. Your stories can conquer worlds if you dedicate them to the right people. Most people here won't listen to you when you tell your stories. Your own wife is staring into the tube enjoying one of the many soap operas while you try to tell her a story to get her opinion. You've been together for forty years and you think it's the right thing to do. But secretly you know something is wrong. Her flesh is as withered as your own. Yet, there is the young widow in the village who hangs on your lips when you tell your stories. You realised it long ago, but your morals forbid you to notice, and yet you secretly dream of her."

I slumped like a heap of misery, this rogue had seen through me. But out of this misery I was seized by lust. I thought of this woman and a pleasant shiver ran through me. He was right, I was wasting my talent on the many ignoramuses, but down there a beautiful woman was rolling around in bed, longing for my stories and for me. I felt a lust that made my body tremble.

"Go down," the devil triumphed, "you'll find her camp ready for you, she'll pine for your stories ... and for you".

My body trembled with desire, but then my head pounded:

You old lecher, what do you want from this young woman, in ten years you really will be an old man, perhaps frail. Maybe so weak that you won't even be able to tell a story. She will still crave interesting men, but you will no longer be able to give her that. Do you really think this woman will still be there for you then?

The devil read my thoughts and intervened:

"Only the moment counts. Do you really want to live a boring life for the next ten years and then spend the rest of your life being just as boring? I can only advise you to live these ten years full of pleasure and joy and not give a damn about what comes after that. Maybe it will even be twenty, nobody knows. You still have so much time."

'No,' I said, 'that would be wrong. Today I'm indulging in lust, and tomorrow I'll be a nursing case and have to be ashamed of this woman. My conscience will torment me because I have spoilt what could have been her best years. Or she will leave me to save herself and will feel guilty because she left me alone in misery. I can't let that happen. My wife and I once promised each other before God until death do us part. Splendid children have come from this union. Should I question all this just because you are fuelling lust in me? I must resist the offer, however tempting it may be. You will lose your power over me."

Now the devil became angry and showed his true colours.

"You old, calcified fool," he roared, "you don't know what's good for you. Go downstairs and tell your stories to the good-for-nothing people. Make a fool of yourself trying to argue against the TV noise. I'll tell you one thing: if you don't manage to turn off the TV in a single pub by midnight tonight, you won't survive this day. Make up your mind now. Either you go down to that young woman and get pleasure and lust for the indefinite future, or you go down to your pathetic stage and breathe your last at midnight if you don't manage to get this decadent people on your side."

It was not only because I detest ultimatums that I decided to forgo short-lived lustful adventures and place my salvation in the lap of the muses. I fervently proclaimed to the devil:

"I'll find the place where people switch off the TV and listen to my stories. Grab yourself, you monster, and don't show your face again until I haven't fulfilled your condition. Otherwise, never show your face again, neither in my lifetime nor on my dying day."

Now the devil had no more power over me, and with a terrible curse he disappeared. I could only hear him growling:

"I'll see you at midnight."

I was alone again, and after the strong promise I had made to the devil, doubt rose up in me, stronger than before. I feared that I had made the wrong decision. Everything I saw on my journey fuelled my doubts. It seemed that hardly anyone wanted to listen when you had something to say. The droning television alone stifled the possibility.

But then I remembered Kiltimagh, Joyce's Bar

here, where I had been so kindly welcomed and listened to a year ago. I was convinced that life here hadn't changed completely in a year. I believe it was also because of you that I had the strength to resist the devil so marvellously. I got on the bus in Donegal and an old friend picked me up in Castlebar. I came straight here to see you. I thank God that the wheel of time didn't turn so quickly with you and I thank you for welcoming me back so kindly and listening to me so carefully. I am convinced that the devil will bite his teeth out of you.

* * *

Thanks to you, I have now put this rogue in his place forever and ever. We will sit together and tell each other stories for all eternity. Thank you all! Sláinte!

Pádraig raises his pint glass and nods to the group. Out of the corner of his eye, Saóirse sees Paul secretly hide a portable television under the bar.

Thunderous applause fills the room. People crowd around Pádraig and pat him on the back. Saóirse, however, is lost in thought, thinking about this story. Despite the noise, her mind is working:

'Did he follow his heart? He resisted lust, but wasn't it the mind that did it?'

Máire pokes her in the ribs and says:

"Don't be gloomy, we're having a good time here and the narrator's story was once again masterful."

"Do you think it was just a story?"

"What does that mean?" laughs Máire, "A story is something alive. In this story, Pádraig met the devil in the flesh."

She stretches her eyes with her fingers, spreads her mouth with her thumbs and shouts: "Boo!"

It looks so funny that Saóirse suddenly has to laugh. They both giggle in a silly way. They chat amusingly, or rather Saóirse doesn't have to say anything, Máire has so much to tell her new friend that Saóirse doesn't have time to say anything about herself. They have a few more 7Up and before Saóirse knows it, the clock reads twenty-three. She has to go to church soon. Then the snack vendor enters the bar. His gaze wanders round the bar and lingers on her. He smiles at her and nods. Saóirse's blood rushes to her head and she thinks she is going to die as he approaches her.

"Hi Seán," Máire calls out to him, "on the prowl?"

Saóirse thinks he sees Seán's face turn a little red. With an embarrassed smile, he says to Saóirse:

"Nice to see you again," then he turns his attention

to a couple of larking about boys, seemingly uninterested in her, but his gaze keeps wandering back to Saóirse. She feels uncomfortable in her own skin and is almost glad that she has to leave soon. Máire whispers softly:

"A cute boy, unfortunately he's after every skirt, watch out."

Saóirse is horrified by what is said and an unfamiliar, painful feeling rises up inside her. She hastily stands up and says:

"I have to go, they're waiting for me."

Máire looks at her in amazement:

"But it's still over half an hour until midnight."

"I know, but maybe my father will come early."

Máire stands up, hugs Saóirse and kisses her on the lips.

"See you tomorrow? An old storyteller is coming. She's said to be several hundred years old. They say she has the face."

"Of course," smiles Saóirse, "I'll be here tomorrow at the same time. I would be delighted to meet you."

The two embrace once more, then she storms out of the pub, Seán's gaze behind her. The streets are still

full of people and Saóirse hurries to the church.
Twenty minutes before midnight, she stands in
front of the deserted church. Sure enough, a quarter
to midnight, her father's car turns up.

Although Saóirse's head is spinning from all the
new impressions, she soon falls into a deep sleep at
home. She dreams of Pádraig and the devil. But
when she wakes up in the bright sunlight, she can't
remember anything. At midday, Saóirse walks back
up the road to the village. She meets a few people,
but no-one she can remember from yesterday. She
is relieved when she sees that the Burger Stubc is
closed. There aren't as many people on the street
today as there were yesterday. There are no young
people outside Joyce's Bar today, even though the
pub seems to be open. But she doesn't dare go in
alone. She strolls past towards the end of the town
until the road forks. She decides to turn right and
cross the little bridge, as she has never been here
before, not even with her brothers.

She comes to a monument where the road forks
again. She decides to take the right again, a narrow
road. Only a few houses are still standing here.
Saóirse feels a deep happiness in her heart. She
really is all alone and nobody knows where she is.
She has never felt this freedom in her short life, and
the warm sun of this August day intensifies the
feeling even more.

'It's probably still too early for the hustle and bustle in the village,' she thinks. That's just as well, because the feelings of those moments would have remained hidden from her for today.

She comes to an old, abandoned house, behind which she has to decide on a path again. Here she is overcome by the fear of getting lost and looks back the way she came. In the distance, she sees the familiar range of hills across in front of her. The Nephin is clearly recognisable in the distance on the right. This image is familiar to her and she now knows that she won't get lost. She continues on her way, quickly climbing the small incline and stopping again and again to let her gaze wander southwards into the distance. She tries to get her bearings and realises that the road she sees half a mile to the south must be the road to Kilkelly. She feels the pride of the nomad girl, who has an innate ability to orientate herself.

She strides forward with much more confidence and is no longer fazed when the road meanders a little and leads steeply downhill. Before her lies a melancholy landscape, a valley, a river. Saóirse knows that it is the River Glore, into which even the salmon that swim up the River Moy via Killala Bay and come here from there sometimes stray. She walks reverently down into the valley. Saóirse loves the Glore, which has no lobby, and yet it crosses the most beautiful landscapes in Mayo. At the bottom, she crosses the small Glore bridge and decides to climb over the wall and walk westwards along the banks of the river. By now it has become very warm, and when she comes to a shady bush, she sits down on the grass and watches the river flow by. The sound stimulates her imagination and she falls into dreams. Suddenly she wakes up and realises that she must have fallen asleep. It seems to have been only a moment, then she realises from the position of the sun that more time must have passed than she thought. She doesn't bother to remember what she might have dreamt. She is too worried that she has missed something important. She jumps up and hurries back to the bridge wall. She climbs over the wall onto the road and makes her way to Kiltimagh. She has been walking for perhaps ten minutes when she hears a car pull up behind her before she can turn round.

"Hi, Saóirse," says the girl in the back seat, "don't you want to listen to the storyteller's stories tonight? She starts in half an hour. There were already two storytellers this afternoon, but nothing that interested us."

"Hello Máire," she replies to her friend, who has recognised her, "I've been there before, but there was nothing going on."

"It's changing very quickly here," Máire calls through the car window, "we can take her into town, can't we, Collin?"

The driver replies: "No problem!"

"Is that really not a problem?" asks Saóirse.

"Nonsense, get in, we'll have as much fun as yesterday."

Saóirse gets in and a few minutes later they pull up outside Joyce's Bar.

Collin says:

"Ladies, here's the show."

The girls get out.

"I'm still looking for a place for the car and I'll be right behind you."

Máire pulls Saóirse into the pub and says casually:

"Collin is nice, but sometimes he drinks too much. Come on, I don't need to introduce you anymore."

Joyce's is even more crowded than yesterday. The babble of voices hits them like a hurricane. Nobody leaves their seat to them today. The empty throne of the storytellers stands majestically in the centre of the pub, nobody dares to take it.

Saóirse's gaze scans the room for the One, but he is not there. Although she is relieved, she feels a disappointment, a disappointment of the kind that is caused by an event that one fears, but for which one has prepared thoroughly, and which then does not materialise. Saóirse doesn't let on and suddenly the chatter stops. After a brief silence, loud applause suddenly fills the room. From the door leading to the back rooms, she makes her way to the chair, the storyteller. Now the girls catch sight of the old woman in the wide, colourful festive dresses of the Travellers. Excited, Máire elbows Saóirse in the side and calls out:

"That's her!"

Saóirse is petrified.

Old Méabh ascends the throne, looks Saóirse abruptly in the eye for a moment and places a finger on her lips. Slowly, the tension in Saóirse 's body eases and gives way to happiness and security. Now they are conspiring here, she and the old Méabh. 'Will I know the story?

The girl who followed the call of her heart

As you all know," she begins, "I am very old, and I would like to tell you about an incident that my great-grandmother experienced a long time ago in Cill Aodain, even before the poet Anthony Raftery was born there. She was a young woman then. Today's Bohola Road was not yet a proper road, and even National Road 5 was a track on which two covered wagons could hardly travel side by side. The town of Kiltimagh as you know it today didn't exist yet, but the cluster of houses, the fact that there was already a church here and that crafts were flourishing were a sure sign that a town would one day be built here. Back then, they parked their caravans not far from where Bohola 's three pubs are today. My great-grandmother also had what they call the face back then and she set off for Kiltimagh with a back basket full of goods and her art to offer to the people there. The journey from Bohola to Kiltimagh took half a morning. She set off at around two o'clock in the afternoon.

On the way to Kiltimagh you passed Cill Aodain. There was a thatched cottage on the left-hand side of the road that was rumoured to be haunted. Nobody liked to use the term haunted house, because it was still inhabited by an old woman and her great-granddaughter. The old woman had not been to Kiltimagh for more than ten years because, as we now know, she could no longer walk well due to arthritis and could not afford an oxcart or even a horse and cart. They grew everything they needed for their meagre existence on their stony land. Four goats and a few chickens provided occasional diversion and the necessary bartering to procure the few essentials that they could not produce themselves. Three times a week, the now seventeen-year-old great-granddaughter set off with a small handcart to sell eggs and goat's cheese at the market in Kiltimagh. So far, so common, because at that time many people in the neighbourhood of the village earned their living in a similar way. What got people in the village whispering were some strange circumstances and occurrences that they didn't know how to categorise in their own village world. The old lady had never been very talkative, but since she stopped coming to Kiltimagh herself, they had hardly seen more than half a dozen villagers around her house, let alone spoken to her. The great-granddaughter had never heard anyone speak a single word, for she had been mute since her mother's early death, even before she could utter her first words. Although the girl could not speak, she was by no means deaf, so she understood what was being said. The muteness was associated with the alleged sacrileges in the house. The circumstances of the mother's death were never really clarified, but as there was no father for this child, there was talk of a curse that had befallen the sinful mother and her bastard. Completing the mystery surrounding the little cottage in Cill Aodain was an observation made by a farmer and his wife as they drove their oxcart from Bohola to Kiltimagh on All Saints' night. They had set off from Bohola in the late afternoon, for the transcendent things I am about to tell you about rarely reveal themselves before nightfall. At this time of year, it was already dawning around five o'clock. As they drove half-asleep along the little lane to the cottage in Cill Aodain, they noticed a bright, unnatural light, like that of a solarium or a television set today, only much brighter. It shone so outrageously that it lit up the road to Coillte Mách for miles and changed the colours of nature so much that they thought they were walking through hell. You can imagine that their hearts almost stopped, as such a colour of light was unheard of at the time. How happy they were when they were finally able to return to the protective cover of darkness. Their curiosity about the source of this terrible light was not great, as they drove their ox as if Satan himself was after them.

That very night, news of this event spread throughout the village. From then on, people only talked about it when they mentioned Cill Aodain. When the girl offered her wares at the market for the first time after this event, nobody wanted to deal with her. The sad girl was about to make her way home without having achieved anything when a man of about fifty with flaming red hair approached her carriage. In the village he was known only as Godless Tom. He lived alone high up in the mountains and nobody really knew what he was doing; people avoided him. Mothers put their arms protectively around their children when they met him. Tom had never hurt anyone, but the fact that he didn't like to talk and was never seen in church made him scary to people.

"I'll take everything you're carrying," said Tom, "I just can't carry it home. If you come with me in your car, I'll give you what you need, I have everything in the house."

The girl nodded and they both set off for the

mountains. You can imagine that this set the rumour mill churning. The villagers feared that something terrible was about to befall the village, as they saw this incident as a link to evil. When the girl was later seen happily travelling through the village towards Cill Aodain with a cart full of cloth, salt, flour and many other goods, the villagers gathered in the church once more than usual during the day to pray against the burgeoning evil. Soon it was felt that praying alone was no longer enough, and the idea of a crusade against evil was no longer only uttered behind closed doors.

In the time that followed, Godless Tom descended from his mountains more and more often to visit the old woman and her great-granddaughter in Cill Aodain. Soon he and the girl were seen walking hand in hand along the Coillte path or in the mountains. When the girl went down to the village with the handcart, she no longer took her goods to the market as she used to, but pulled it to the end of the village and then into the mountains. She was often only seen walking in the opposite direction the next day with bartered goods. It was said that godless Tom and the girl had a sinful relationship, and there was no doubt that God would punish them both, just as he had punished the girl's mother. A new calamity would befall them and the old woman who tolerated it.

Then fate struck. Misfortune struck the girl in her nineteenth year, a stroke of fate that shrouded the entire village in an embarrassed silence, filling many eyes with tears, eyes that not so long ago would have preferred to see the girl slain under the curse of God."

Old Méabh takes a long break here. The silence in the pub is as thick as cold flour sauce. She casts a glance round, looks at many an embarrassed face and then continues with a tension you can feel.

"When my great-grandmother arrived, it was already too late. Although she had already mastered many medical arts, she could only offer the girl her lap and bless her before her soul left her body forever and ended her suffering. Her clothes were torn and soaked with blood. She wrapped the battered body in one of the bales of cloth she had brought with her to cover the gaping wounds. A six-year-old boy and his sister, who was a year older, sat by the wayside, distraught and crying. As she bandaged their relatively minor wounds, she struggled to reconstruct what had happened from the fragments they were tearfully recounting, interrupted time and again by convulsive crying.

The children had been playing in the field in the afternoon and were on their way back to the village at dusk. Suddenly, two large black dogs appeared out of nowhere and pounced on the brother and sister without making a sound. Just as the children were thrown to the ground, the mute girl, who was on her way to Cill Aodain with her handcart, came running round the next bend in the road, screaming loudly. She had left her handcart behind because she sensed mortal danger when she heard the children's screams. With its bare hands, it lunged at one of the black beasts standing directly above the boy. As it grabbed the beast by the ears with all its might, it let go of him and pounced on the brave girl. Lying on the ground, she fought with the overpowering opponent as if possessed. The second beast had also let go of the sister and pounced on the girl. The black devils were bent on an unquenchable bloodlust. Then the siblings heard the mute girl shout the only words that had ever been heard by a human: "Run, children, run as fast as you can!"

The dogs had already let go of their dying victim when my great-grandmother arrived," says the narrator. Then she continues:

"She took the dead heroine's handcart and drove her the short distance to Cill Aodain. The two children, still distraught, accompanied her. When the old woman saw her dead great-granddaughter, she remained calm.

"Something has been prophesied," she said, "on the night of All Saints' Day her mother appeared to us, we both saw her. She said that Saóirse would meet her father, who lived in the mountains of Kiltimagh. They were to spend a short, happy time together before an event that would plunge the whole village into deep mourning would bring Saóirse to her forever. The first words she would ever speak would also be her last.

The old Méabh pauses for a moment, looks round with her wise eyes and continues:

"Here ends the story of the girl who followed her heart, even if it led her to her death. With her courageous act, she won the hearts of people whose lack of understanding and ignorance had already condemned this girl. Well," the old woman concludes her story with a twinkle in her eye, "the people of Kiltimagh have of course learnt their lesson from these events. I've never heard anyone in this town say anything bad about someone before they really know them. But in our tribe, every generation since that event, we've named a girl after the silent heroine who, as hard as it was, followed her heart at the crucial moment."

Saóirse was very moved, she suddenly realised that the old Méabh had only told her this story, the others in the pub were just a backdrop. She hardly noticed the enthusiastic applause that began after a short pause. Old Méabh's words kept running through her mind:

The call of the heart is very quiet, but the way the girl acted at the crucial moment, her heart must have really been screaming, louder than her mind. Her mind would have told her: stay out of this, you have no chance. These and other thoughts ran through her head. The mute heroine, her namesake, came back to her mind, would she also have thrown herself so bravely at this black beast? The mere thought of such a bloodthirsty monster made her shudder and she had to painfully admit to herself that she would not have had the courage. She felt sad and ashamed, wasn't Old Méabh overestimating her capabilities?

Without Saóirse noticing her approach, she hears the old woman's voice say to her:

"Remember that the great ocean is made up of many small drops. It's not a few big things that make up a life, but the many small ones, so don't be too hard on yourself."

The old woman seems to have guessed her thoughts again, smiling as she turns away and leaves the pub, many eyes following her.

"What did she tell you?" asks Máire curiously and almost a little jealously. Saóirse just repeats the bit about the ocean.

"She must be very wise," nods Máire approvingly, "is she really several hundred years old?"

"You can rely on that," says Saóirse confidently. The old woman's words have done her good and her self-doubt has disappeared.

Saóirse gathers from snippets of conversation that the people here are still preoccupied with the fate of the mute girl. Opinions differ as to whether something like this really could have happened in Cill Aodain a long time ago. Whether true or not, it seems to preoccupy the people here.

"There's a storyteller coming soon who I don't know yet," says Máire, "she's supposed to be very good and from Sligo. Let's have another drink and wait for her."

Saóirse agrees and is looking forward to the next story. They fool around a little and don't realise that the storyteller is already among them. Then Paul rings a bell and everyone realises that the storyteller is coming, who no one here knows yet.

"Today I would like to introduce you to a young master storyteller who I met in Sligo Town and who I definitely didn't want to keep from you," Paul begins in his deep, deliberate bass voice. "This is Adeen O Carroll and she's also from Sligo. At only twenty-nine, she's a brilliant storyteller. Please Adeen, I'd like you to take the storyteller's throne," Paul points with both hands to the raised chair in the centre of the pub. Right next to Saóirse and Máire, a young woman makes her way through the crowd and climbs onto the chair. Nobody would have thought she was a storyteller, she is wearing normal clothes, a blouse and jeans. An astonished murmur goes through the crowd, she was an unusual appearance on this chair. Paul brings her a glass of Smithwick's. Suddenly it is as quiet as a mouse.

"Yes, I'm a beer-drinking woman, but don't worry, I'm not Dicey Reilly," she begins with a twinkle in her eye and a strong alto voice. Everyone knows Dicey Reilly and they laugh.
"I want to tell you a story that, as true as I am sitting here, I have experienced myself. I think you'll believe me now; we'll see if you still believe me after the story. The girl in the story is called, not surprisingly, Adeen. But I'm going to tell it from a distance. I've called this story "The Hole in the Wall", and you'll soon see why.

The hole in the wall

In a small town in Sligo, the little girl Adeen lives with her father and her two older brothers. Six months ago, when Adeen was still five years old, her mother died after a serious illness. She was the best mum anyone could have and the little girl can't understand why she should never come home again. Mum has been gone for so long and she longs for her very much. How often have she and Dad sat alone in the parlour, talking and crying about Mum, she knows that Dad misses her too. But she often sits alone in her room and thinks of happy times. Mum loved to laugh and Adeen often remembers her laughter. On Sundays after church, Mum would prepare lunch and they would all sit around the big kitchen table and have a great time. Mum had always kept the family together.

Today, they all more or less go their own ways and on Sundays she usually goes to her favourite aunt for dinner. She gave her comfort during the hardest times, but she couldn't replace Mum either.

Adeen is home alone today and she is very hot. She has half-laid down on her bed and is looking at the squiggles in the wallpaper pattern. After a while, they start to dance and, as so often happens, the time when Mum was still there comes alive before her eyes. She remembers how she combed her hair and put clips in it, how she showed her how to tie her shoes. She remembers tender hugs and kisses when Mum said goodbye to her for pre-school. It's as if a film is playing on the wall and the squiggles dance and circle in between.

But then Adeen realises that they are all circling around a single small vortex and her eyes fix on it. Soon the circling rings on the wall become blurred and a hole appears in the centre of the vortex. It is black at first, then the darkness contracts and all around it is now as blue as the sky. Adeen stares spellbound at the hole, which is slowly getting bigger, and now she can see a blue eye in the centre. She should be frightened, but the eye looks at her lovingly. Then Adeen realises that it is Mum's eye. The swirls gradually disappear into the edge and now Mum's smiling face appears, first her head and then she stands in the room in full size. Adeen's little heart is pounding with joyful excitement, she has finally come back. She is wearing a white apron, the one she used to wear on Sundays when she prepared lunch.

Adeen jumps up from her bed and throws herself into her arms. Mum hugs her tightly and kisses her forehead.

"My brave little girl," says Mum, "I know how much you missed me, but I couldn't show myself to you any sooner. But I was always with you when you thought of me."

"But now you must never, ever leave me again," Adeen shouts, "if only Dad were here, he misses you so much too."

Mum's face looks kind and serious as she says:

 "I know, my child. But now I'm here to explain everything to you. I want you to understand and I have to ask you to be very brave. I'm also going to visit Dad and your brothers; they have to be brave too."

Adeen's heart sinks and she knows it must really be her when Mum says it.

"Trust me," says Mum, "once you've understood everything, it won't be so bad."

Adeen decides not to let her down, because she trusts her.

Mum takes her by the hand and walks straight through the wall with her. At first it is dark; Adeen feels Mum's hand and is not afraid. Then it gets brighter and brighter and a little later they find themselves in a fresh green meadow with lots of colourful flowers. The sun is high in the sky and shines down on them bright and friendly. Mum stops and says:

"This is a hospitable place, let's rest here."

She sits down on the grass and has Adeen sit down with her back to her. She hugs her daughter from behind and folds her arms around her small shoulders. Then she begins very gently:

"Have you ever noticed that all things, flowers, animals and even people come, stay for a while and then leave again?"

She looks around and points to a bright red flower.

"This beautiful, proud poppy grew from a single seed."

Then she points to a bud of the same flower.

"She's still young, like you. She hasn't really seen the world yet. But soon she will be like her older sister, bright red and radiantly beautiful. The bees and other insects will praise her beauty, visit her and enjoy her hospitality. But soon she will weaken and then shed her beautiful dress."

She grabs the stem of a wilted poppy flower, the

last leaves falling off as she plucks it. She shows it to Adeen and continues:

"It was born, grew and blossomed proudly and beautifully like the one I have just shown you. Now its time is over and the flower has died. Now you can say: "That's sad", but in reality, it's not, because it didn't live in vain, but fulfilled an important task. She takes the flower basket in both hands and breaks it apart. She rubs one half between her fingers and small fibres become visible; she shows them to Adeen and says:

"The mother has left behind many little children and from each of these seeds a new flower can grow. In order for the proud flowers to bloom again next year, the old ones must die. In truth, dying is nothing more than preparation for living on. So we need not be sad if this flower has died here, because it will produce many new ones.

However, this not only applies to these flowers, but also to trees, animals and, ultimately, humans. Each species has its own rhythm of life and even within species, some live shorter and others longer. Of all the species of life, we humans are special because we have the ability to think about our lives. Look, you are still small and don't know that much yet, but you already know that you are here. You know more than all the animals and plants. Although you are only five years old, you know more than a fifty-year-old elephant or a two-hundred-year-old tortoise. Everything you see, smell, taste and feel was once created from the dust of this earth, the plants, the animals and the people. The dust of this earth was created from the sun a long, long time ago, and the sun is only a small part of a widely scattered heap that was once a large whole. When you look at the sun or at the stars at night, you see the dust of the stars from which you too were created. So you can look up into the sky and say: That's me.

No living person knows how all this came about, some say it has always been there and others speak of a big bang in which the stardust was created and from which the star clusters, called galaxies, were formed. Still others speak of God who created the stardust. Whichever of these is correct, perhaps there is a fourth or fifth possibility that we humans do not yet know, it is all fantastic and amazing. A world that has created itself is just as possible or impossible as creation by God. Actually, people should walk around with their mouths open all day and their entire lives because they can't stop marvelling. But in reality, only a few are amazed. A child still marvels at everything that happens around it, but adults have forgotten how to do so. They take everything for granted, although most of them don't understand what is happening around them, they simply don't think about it. They see the sun and the stars and don't even marvel at them, even though they don't know how they get there or what keeps them there. Go down to the city and say:

"I come from the sun and the stars", the younger children will certainly be curious to hear more about it, the older children might laugh at you and adults might smile at you. Only a few will realise that you are right. So most people live their whole lives in a twilight sleep. They take their unimportant little things seriously; they worship their possessions and money. But they don't realise that they are looking into their own past when they look up into the sky. Nevertheless, there have always been people who have looked into the sky and recognised the secret. There are examples of some who gave up all possessions when they woke up from the great general twilight sleep.

Only sometimes in life does everyone experience the breath of eternity, namely when a loved one passes away. Many have woken up from such an experience and never gone back to sleep.

You, my little girl, had to feel the breath of eternity very early on, namely on the day when eternity called me to itself. I didn't leave you voluntarily, because we humans don't have a choice. But I don't want you, like most people, to simply fall asleep again and spend the rest of your life in a state of twilight until eternity calls you too.

I have come back to give you another little glimpse so that you can go through life with an alert mind for the rest of what is sure to be a long life. Never forget the wonder that is still yours as a child. Remain self-confident and don't let the sleepers dissuade you when you say: "I come from the sun and the stars."

If people laugh about it, they are stupid because they don't understand it.

I'm going to tell you the most important thing now, and my greatest wish is that you understand. I have actually been sent to bring you to me in eternity. But I want you to go through that hole back into life, you still have so much to learn before I wait for you here again. I told you that you have to be brave, because I can't go with you. I already have my place in heaven where I will return. One day, however, we will be reunited. The time may seem long to you, but in eternity it is not even a moment. I will stand at the gate and pick you up, and then we will never part again. Always remember that when you think you miss me. There will come a time when your life will be full of joy and you won't even miss me because you will feel that I am in your heart."

Mum rises from the grass and takes Adeen by the hand. Her face smiles with a beauty and love that Adeen herself has never seen before.

"Come on, my brave little girl," she says, "Dad and all your loved ones are waiting for you, I'll take you to the gate. Tell them I love them all and they needn't worry."

They leave the colourful meadow and walk towards a dark hole. Mum stops and smiles lovingly at Adeen:

"You have to get through this, and remember that I will be waiting for you here one day in the distant future. I know you are a clever girl and will go through life with your eyes wide open. You came from the sun and the stars and will return there one day, don't look back."

Adeen does what Mum says. When she goes into the dark hole, everything seems to spin around her. She closes her eyes and recognises the doctor's voice saying:

"She's over it, the fever has gone down."

When she opens her eyes, everyone she loves is standing by her bed, Dad is sitting on it and has taken her little hands in his. His eyes are full of tears, but there is a smile on his face.

"Why are you crying, Dad? I went to see Mum, but she couldn't come with me. She loves you all and you shouldn't worry."

The father picks Adeen up, hugs her tightly and whispers in her ear:

"I know, my brave little girl. You have returned from eternity. One day we'll all be there with Mum. But for now, I'm glad you'll be with us for a very, very long time."

This is where Adeen's story ends.

"Thank you very much for your attention. I would also like to add that Mum actually visited Dad and comforted him. You can ask my dad, he also talks openly about it. He's still with us and we often talk about Mum. My brothers didn't talk to me about it, but if Mum told me, then she did. I don't ask about it either, everyone deals with their losses differently - it's the most personal thing in the world. For me, the most beautiful vision of heaven is that one day you will be reunited with all your loved ones there.

I hope and wish that one or two people who have already suffered such a loss can draw comfort from my story. Once again, thank you all!"

It remained as quiet as a mouse throughout the presentation, which lasted for quite a while. Not even orders were placed during the lecture. Then the applause suddenly erupted and rolled through the restaurant like a dam bursting. Saóirse and Máire wipe the tears from their eyes that they couldn't suppress. There is no doubt in their minds that this story happened. In fact, it is based on a true story.

Everyone agrees that it was a special story that cannot be compared with the others. It takes a while for the normal hustle and bustle to get going again. The narrator is standing at the bar with a couple of young people, chatting happily over a pint. You could ask her about her story and she was very open about it. She knows that one day her mum will embrace her again.

It's getting late and Saóirse's free time for the week is coming to an end. Then she sees Seán coming out of a group of boys, she hadn't even noticed him. He makes his way through the densely packed bodies and comes straight towards her. Her knees go weak, a feeling she had never experienced before. She would like to disappear on the spot;

then he is with her.

"Isn't your name Saóirse too, like the girl in the story before last?" The blood rushes to her face and she nods sheepishly.

"And mute like our heroine," he teases her.

"Fuck off," says Máire, "there's nothing to get here, I've told the girl about you."

"Could you mind your own business for a change?" Seán responds, a little annoyed.

"Girl gossip, don't listen to her," he says, turning to Saóirse, "I know I have a bad reputation, but I don't mind as long as people don't get in my way."

"Saóirse is under my protection, so I'll get in your way," Máire replies unperturbed. Seán takes no notice of her.

"I want to go on a date with you," he says to Saóirse. She plucks up all her courage and hears herself say it:

"Will you be at the snack bar next Saturday?"

"Next Saturday?" he asks, slightly irritated, "That's almost a week away, I'm currently there every day from one o'clock, except Sundays."

"Next Saturday," Saóirse insists, "you can make me a proposal then."

"All right, Saturday at my place." He smiles at her and leaves the pub immediately, which relieves Saóirse, because she had plucked up all her courage for this appointment. She couldn't bear to look at him again now.

"I can only warn you," says Máire, visibly worried, "you don't know everything about him, he's playing tricks on the girls. Those who don't know him are crazy about him, he's good-looking, so they don't realise what a bad person he is. He always has several girlfriends at the same time, in Dublin, where he studies, here, in this neighbourhood. In Balla, he treated a girl very badly."

"Stop it," says Saóirse, annoyed, "I want to see for myself, there's so much talk."

"You're about to fall for him, you won't be happy with him. Once he's had you, he'll drop you like a hot potato."

"If," Saóirse replied, "I don't want to talk about it now. By the way, it's already twenty minutes to midnight, I have to hurry." She kisses Máire left and right on the cheek and says goodbye:

"Thanks for your company, I'll see you next week." She turns to the door and leaves. When she arrives at the church, her father is already waiting for her.

The week is becoming unbearably long for Saóirse.

She impatiently longs for Saturday, even though there is a little sting in her soul. The seeds of mistrust have been sown, the only question is whether they will sprout. But the desire to see Seán again is stronger and pushes the slightly bitter taste into the background.

It's finally Saturday again, and Saóirse's anticipation is undimmed. No one had ever asked her about her experiences before, not out of disinterest, but to give her the opportunity to process everything without being influenced. When she needed advice, she turned to her parents or to the old Méabh, they knew that. But now, when Saóirse gives her father a kiss and wants to get out, he asks with a smile:

"Do you have a date?" She blushes as she says:

"I don't know, I think so."

"Only do what you really want, if you have any doubts, don't do it."

"Yes, Dad," she says, "thank you." She gives him another kiss on the cheek and gets out.

Now the time has come and she can feel the excitement. The streets are bustling with normal activity, housewives are shopping, tractors are driving through the town, men in work clothes are crossing the road to have lunch at the coffee shop or the Cill Aodain Hotel. Some young lads greet her with "How are you, Saóirse?", it seems she knows more people here than she realises. It's an unpleasant fact that it's so easy to remember a stranger's name. But it's hardly possible to recognise everyone in such a short time. You usually know that, but you still have the feeling that you should have returned a greeting by name. You constantly feel on the defensive.

When Saóirse reaches the burger snack bar, she pauses for a moment in front of the window and looks in. Seán has already seen her and comes running to the door with a cheerful laugh. Saóirse thinks he looks very handsome in his white apron.

"Come in," he smiles and holds out his hand to her. She grabs it and follows him into the back room.

"It's nice that you're here so early, there's not so much going on at this time of day, so we can have a little chat," and he adds almost casually, "I've been looking forward to seeing you." She blushes as she says this:

"Me too." Then his face turns serious as he says:

"Your girlfriend has been here twice this week and asked me to leave you alone. What did she tell you about me?"

After a short pause, Saóirse answers:

"Nothing really, I didn't want to know anything."

"You shouldn't believe everything either, there's a lot of talk here."

"I suppose," says Saóirse, "if there's something important to say about you, you'll tell me yourself. For the rest, you don't have to answer to me, we hardly know each other."

"It's nice that you see it that way," replies Sèan, "but I want you to know the truth and not what's being said about me." Saóirse makes a defensive gesture:

"I won't be told anything, let's get to know each other first before you defend yourself, even though I'm not attacking you. I don't want to be confused by rash confessions. I want to see you through my own eyes, not yours or anyone else's."

Seán's face brightens again:

"Thank you, that's fair enough, in your eyes I'm as innocent as a child, this is a chance I haven't had in a long time."

When three children come in from the street, he kisses Saóirse on the lips and says:

"I'm busy here until eight o'clock, let's continue talking in the Raftery Room, I'll be there right after work."

"Fine," she says with a smile, "but no confession. I've heard you're studying in Dublin; I'd like to know more about that."

"Okay," he says, "tonight then."

The girl leaves the pub without turning round again, now she really does have something of a rendezvous. As she still has plenty of time before then, she decides to follow the path of the mute heroine to Cill Aodain. She has often thought about the story of the old Méabh, and the heroic deed of her namesake is etched in her memory. She wants to see the place where the house of the old woman and her mute great-granddaughter stood. She also wants to go round the bend in the road that the mute girl ran round to save her siblings from the clutches of the stray beasts. She crosses the town and runs up Bohola Road. After about an hour, she reaches Cill Aodain. The road takes a sharp left turn, while straight ahead a wide path leads up to a two-storey, currently uninhabited house. It is unlikely to have stood in the years of the events described here; it is perhaps thirty years old. But this bend is probably the decisive one, because the next bend only comes after we have left Cill Aodain. Saóirse looks to the right for any sign of the cottage, but there is nothing to be seen. She stops at the spot where she suspects the cottage once stood; the Méabh's story had given an exact description, so she is convinced that she is standing where the house once stood.

Saóirse listens reverently into the land, as if expecting to catch a sign of the past. She almost thinks she hears the girl's determined screams as she lunged at the black beast, but it is only the wailing of the wind.

She still has plenty of time and sits down in the cushion of thick grass, which is quite high here. She has closed her eyes. Her other senses are focussed on nature. The scent of wild flowers and grasses, the occasional whine of light gusts of wind and their gentle stroking of her face, the chirping and singing of birds, the chirping of cicadas, the rustling of small mammals and lizards in the grass. Only occasionally does the sound of a car reach her ears. Then she remembers the story of the boy who was looking for his shadow, which old Méabh had told around the campfire some time ago.

The boy who sought his shadow

The boy, Andrew McDonagh, lived in a cottage in the mountains of Donegal. One day, on his 18th birthday, he realised that he was different from his peers. He had no shadow. This was well known and he had been a loner and outsider for a long time, but until now it hadn't bothered him. The realisation that he was different hit him out of the blue. He was shunned, he sat alone on his bench at school and the chair next to him remained empty. It was almost as if they were afraid of him. Other outsiders were teased, but he wasn't given as much attention. It was as if he didn't even exist.

Andrew left school at the top of his class, but when he looked for work, the owners of the few local companies found many excuses to turn him away. So he stayed at home and looked after the garden. Now everything was different, he felt lonely and abandoned, his mum was his only human contact.

"Why don't I have a shadow like the others?" he asked at the lonely birthday table.

Her mother shrugged her shoulders and replied: "I can't tell you that. You were born with it like everyone else, but it was taken away from you when you were little."

"Who?" cried the boy desperately.

"I can't tell you that, my boy. You have to accept it as it is." His mother took his hand and continued.

"Leave the others, I love you and I don't mind that you don't have a shadow."

Andrew became very angry and pulled his mum's hand away. He jumped up, ran up and down the room and shouted:

"I can't go on living like this. I have to go away and find my shadow."

The mother shrugged her shoulders again and said:

"I can't and won't stop you, do what you have to do. But don't expect me to support you, you're on your own out there. Don't blame me later."

Andrew didn't answer and didn't think about it for long. He went to his room and packed up his things. When he went to kiss his mum goodbye, she turned away and turned her cheek to him.

"I hope you know what you're doing," she said.

Andrew left the house without turning round again. He walked down the village street and felt relieved when he left the village exit sign behind him. He had walked many kilometres before he began to think about his journey. They wouldn't know him in the next village. He knew how to do it so that his flaw wouldn't be noticed. His heart leapt as he thought of all the new opportunities that were now open to him. But worry also crept into his heart. How was he supposed to find his shadow, he didn't have the slightest idea.

The sun was low as he crossed the city limits. It was the time of the long shadows and he was glad that he didn't meet anyone here. When he reached the town centre, he decided to look for a job first, as he had only brought a few pounds with him from home.

There was a garden centre in the town and, as he knew a lot about gardening, he went there and spoke to the owner. He showed her his excellent references and told her about his skills. The boss took a liking to him and gave him a room, board and a few pounds a week pocket money. In the time that followed, he proved that he was more than worth the money and, as she wanted to keep him, he was earning something like a proper wage after just six months.

Nobody realised that he had no shadow. In the first few months, he often thought about how he could find it, but as time went on, he forgot about it more and more. The people who met him liked him because he was a nice and polite boy. The girls in the village were soon talking about the handsome gardener's boy.

Everything was fine until one day, probably two years ago, an old man entered the shop. Andrew was working as a shop assistant that day.

"Can I help you?" he asked the old man.

"You have to ask the question the other way round," the old man replied, looking firmly at the boy.

"The question is whether I can help you," the old man continued.

Andrew was embarrassed and realised he was blushing.

"I, I don't understand," he stammered, "what would you want to help me with?"

"So, so," said the old man, "are you really all right?"

Andrew felt a fist clawing at his guts. The old man had recognised him, but how? The light in the shop was so diffuse that no one cast a shadow. Perhaps he meant something else, so he answered cautiously:

"I don't know what."

The old man was still staring at the boy.

"Forgive me," he said, "I haven't introduced myself yet: I am the repression and I have your shadow. When you were a little boy, almost a baby, I was with you and I took him. I was called because he had become a burden to you. He became more and more tormenting for you, so much so that a child as small as you were then could not bear it. When I took him in, you no longer had to suffer. For a long time I had no trouble keeping your shadow, but then you turned eighteen. He became restless and unruly and almost got away from me. Then his rebellion subsided, and after a few months he was tame again and resigned to his fate, until a few days ago when he escaped from me. I'm afraid he'll try to find you, but I see he hasn't been here yet, I'll stay with you and wait for him here, you have nothing to fear if you leave him to me."

Andrew had listened to the old man with great astonishment. For a long time he couldn't say anything, then he pulled himself together.

"Why should I leave him to them?" he asked the old man.

"Why do you ask? Don't you know what awaits you? You will suffer unbearable pain if your shadow reunites with you, perhaps you will even die of agony. Shadows always try to stay united with their owners. This is good as long as the pain does not become too great. But sometimes, like with you, I have to intervene and take it. I take painstaking care that they don't escape from me and harm their former owners. I usually succeed in locking them up for good. The humans may not be happy without him for the rest of their lives, but they don't suffer. But sometimes I have a mishap, like yours, and the dark, cunning thing tries to reunite with its owners. I try to prevent this with all the means at my disposal, after all I am responsible for it. So I must ask you - for your own protection - to allow me to prevent the union. It can be assumed that he is already lurking in the immediate vicinity, but he is still shying away from me."

"I want my shadow back," the boy shouted excitedly, "whatever it does to me, it can't be as bad as the unhappiness I feel when I have to live without it."

"You don't know what you're talking about," the old man hissed, "do you want to die?" The boy replied with the same agitation:

"I'd rather die than be unhappy, even if I've

hardly realised it in the last two years. I would have loved to date a girl, but something stopped me. Now I realise that I was afraid she would notice my flaw. I want my shadow, whatever the cost."

At that moment, the room darkened and Andrew felt something enter him. Suddenly things appeared inside him that he had never noticed before, and they hurt, a lot.

"No!" cried the boy, "you can't do this." He crouched down and began to cry profusely, the tears flowing like rivulets from his eyes.

"That's him," the old man shouted angrily. He lunged at the shadow and tugged at it, trying to pull it to the ground, half succeeding. Andrew crouched on the ground and sobbed, the pain had subsided, he felt empty. But the shadow could no longer be subdued by the old man. As soon as he had escaped, he reached for the boy again, the torment took hold of him anew, the torture was barely bearable until the old man regained control for a short time, then his strength was exhausted.

"Farewell," he called to the boy, "I can't help you now, even if he tortures you to death."

Andrew did not die!

It was painful when the shadow reconnected
with him, but the pain lessened over time. It
took two years for him to fully accept it. From
then on, it accompanied him wherever he went,
it no longer hurt, the wounds were scarred. The
happiness was indescribable, the feeling of
having him as his own. Andrew soon fell in love
with a girl, married her, had children and
became happy with his family. He never let the
old man cross his threshold again.

Saóirse wakes up, she must have fallen asleep. She
remembers Old Méabh saying to her at the end of
the story: 'How lucky for you that the old man
never came to you. But with you, there was never
any reason to take away your shadow. '

A glance at the clock signalled that it was time to
leave, but she could still easily make her way down
to the town. On the street, she turns round once
more and decides to revisit this historic place, then
walks purposefully down into the town.

She arrives at the Raftery Room fifteen minutes
before her appointment and goes straight in. She
walks down the long corridor and enters the back
room. A few men are sitting at the bar in front of
their pints. Many tables are occupied, people are
having dinner here. She recognises some of them
and they wave in a friendly manner when they see

the girl. Saóirse sits down at the front table, which is still free. She puts down her jacket and bag and grabs a Coke from the bar. From her seat, she can see the door. The closer the eight hand gets, the more restless she becomes. Now the big one has reached the top mark, she would like to leave immediately. But another ten long minutes pass and then it is finally Seán who enters. He immediately catches her with his gaze, waves to her and grabs a pint from the bar. With a "Hi Saóirse", he sits down opposite her.

"Have you been waiting long?" he asks. She answers truthfully and briefly recounts her walk up to Cill Aodain.

"A strange place," he says, "full of stories. You won't believe it, but I was sitting there, just like you, remembering a forgotten story that my grandmother told me when I was a child."

Seán pauses meaningfully, then begins to tell Saóirse this story:

The peace-loving warrior and the elves of Coillte Maghach

Long before Kiltimagh was created, the area was covered by a dense forest. It was ruled by an elven queen, and the legend of her beauty has survived to this day. Cill Aodain was the place where this queen resided. Her name was Al'Dórin and her territory stretched from present-day Bohola through Kiltimagh down to Bala and from Swinford to Clairemorris. Many thousands of elves lived here. The only area not colonised by them was Sliabh Cairn, the range of hills in what is now Kiltimagh. These were ruled by the dwarf people Anhàn, whose king was the fierce McOnór. A portal carved into the Sliabh Cairn in the west led to their subterranean realm of Coillte Anhàn, which at the time undermined the entire Sliabh Cairn. Elves and dwarves disliked each other, although in more than four thousand years of coexistence there had never been a war. No dwarf would ever set foot in the forest, because dwarves hated it. Above all, they loved the cool darkness of their caves and no dwarf has ever been found outside in daylight. Elves, on the other hand, are bright creatures who love the light. They had built their dwellings high up in the treetops in order to be as close to the sun as possible. If a human occasionally wandered through the forest, he would not notice the existence of the elves. Humans rarely came here in those days, as the nearest settlement was far away in what is now Castlebar. Elves had the ability to remain completely silent, at least to the ears of humans, as they had the gift of communicating across the entire sound spectrum. To communicate across many miles, they used infrasound below the audible range, which was barely muffled by trees and bushes. For conversations with friends nearby, they used ultrasound. However, if they wanted to, they could also communicate in the sound spectrum audible to humans; they could even speak the language of humans. However, there had never been a conversation between them since the elves had been alive and no one knew whether there had ever been an exchange. Nevertheless, the language of the humans was cultivated, as if they had sensed that this knowledge might become important to them one day in the distant future. The humans back then knew nothing of the existence of the elves. When they roamed the forests to hunt, they had never seen an elf or heard a single sound. But they would have had the chance. Elves, especially the young ones, were sometimes in the mood for jokes. They would exuberantly

sing elven songs in bright tones, which often
sounded like the howling of wind or the chirping
of crickets to humans. Although wind noises are
very unlikely when there is no wind, humans
had not noticed this mischief. This amused the
young elves and they laughed heartily about it.
The dwarves, on the other hand, had rough
throats and were not particularly quiet where
they moved. They were great craftsmen and
turned precious metals, which were still plentiful
in the Sliabh Cairn at the time, into the most
beautiful rings and necklaces. Among them were
talented master builders and skilful smiths for
precious metals and iron. Their kingdom was
lavishly endowed with gold and silver; dwarves
were rich. The most precious metal, however,
was anhánicum, which was very rare and only
found here in the Sliabh Cairn. It was hard, so
hard that a sword made of this metal would cut
through a block of steel like butter. No weapon,
made by man or dwarf, could have pierced
chainmail made of this metal. The metal was
light, so a chain mail shirt weighed little more
than a normal one and a sword no more than a
pencil. It took the dwarves four decades of
digging to extract the ore for exactly one sword
and one piece of chain mail. Now it lay before
them, made for the stature of a human. For there

was a legend that said: One day a great human warrior will come and lead the people of Coillte Anhàn into the mountains of Donegal. A strong, cruel human king ruled there at that time, who had come across the water from the east with a large army and had driven humans and dwarves to Sligo, Galway and Mayo. McOnór's brother O'Gael was driven from there into exile in Coillte Anhàn, where he lived humiliated and waited for the appearance of the great human warrior, for humans and dwarves had a common enemy.

But then things turned out differently. The conqueror of Donegal, whose name was Cal Brighton, mobilised his army to raid the interior of the country. He left a trail of devastation in his wake and no-one could offer him any serious resistance. One day he found himself outside Castlebar. After a fierce battle, the people of Castlebar retreated and fled to Al'Dórin's Forest. From here they hoped to offer resistance from ambush. Cal Brighton occupied Castlebar and moved on towards present-day Bala the very next day. The army set up camp there. Cal Brighton intended to build a fortress here, and from there he initially wanted to hunt down the fugitives from Castlebar. A week later, his men began to clear the forest.

The elves had so far kept out of human disputes because they had already heard of wars among them and that was really their business alone. There were no wars between different elven peoples, they were friends with each other. No sooner had the humans started felling trees than infrasonic voices reported the destruction of elven dwellings on the edge of the realm of Al'Dórin. There had never been an attack like this before and Al'Dórin summoned the Council of Elves.

In the meantime, news of the invasion had spread as far as Coillte Anhàn and McOnór summoned his brother O'Gael and the Anhàn elders.

"The army of Agil Sachá," McOnór began, "the soldiers of Cal Brighton are invincible unless the prophesied human warrior appears soon to take the armour and sword of Anhàn and use them for our benefit."

His brother points out:

"Legend has it that this human warrior will come to lead us against the Agil Sachá in Donegal. But now Cal Brighton's troops are invading our land and there is no sign or sound of this human warrior. We have to ask ourselves whether we want to believe the legend any longer.

An indignant murmur goes through the ranks of the old dwarves. Then McOnór hisses angrily at his brother:

"Those who do not believe in the legend betray our people, watch your tongue, O'Gael, or you are no longer my brother. It may be that we misinterpret the legend, but there is no doubt about it."

O'Gael did not dare to say anything in reply. Then the oldest and wisest of the Anhàn spoke up:

"The human warrior must already be near us, we may just not have recognised him yet. It is perhaps our mistake to wait for a great warrior. An old saying of the elves, sorry my children, but wisdom is not our prerogative alone, so the saying goes: do not seek greatness only in greatness. Perhaps our great warrior is small and that is why we have not yet recognised him."

Silence reigned at first in the assembly hall, then it sounded as if from a single mouth:

"El Gabriel!" El Gabriel is a human child who has lived with the dwarves for fourteen years, a foundling they found abandoned in the forest. He lived inconspicuously among the dwarves

and had since been trained as a master goldsmith
- they had already accepted him as a dwarf. But
El Gabriel, like the dwarves, did not like the
darkness inside the Sliabh Cairn. He knew the
forests of Coillte Maghach and loved them more
than the mountain caves. In his free hours he
roamed them and one day he noticed that the
wind was howling even though there was no
breeze. He knew that something was wrong. The
elf children immediately noticed that El Gabriel
was reacting differently to the other humans
they had teased so far. He lay down on the grass
and closed his eyes. He lay there for an hour
without moving. The elf children became
curious and wanted to see why the boy was
lying there motionless. They carefully climbed
down from their tree to have a look. As elves
moved silently, El Gabriel could not hear their
footsteps, but he recognised their voices. As the
elven children were still inexperienced and only
knew that humans cannot perceive infra- and
ultrasound, they spoke in a high-pitched range
that is not normally accessible to humans. What
they didn't know was that young people, i.e.
children, can hear high-pitched sounds that
adults can no longer perceive. So the boy heard
the elf children chatting. As they leant over him
curiously, El Gabriel suddenly opened his eyes

and laughed in their faces.

"Hello," he said cheerfully, "what beautiful children we have here."

"We are elf children," the girl replied after a brief moment of surprise.

"I've heard about you," said the boy, "you're supposed to be sneaky and mean."

"Rubbish," replied the elf boy, "only the dwarves say that."

"I am a dwarf," said El Gabriel.

"You?" said the elf girl and let out a loud snort, but at such a high pitch that the human boy couldn't hear the laughter.

"Are you a dwarf? Then you're either too long or too thin."

"Besides, dwarves never come into our forest," added the young elf.

"But I'm a dwarf," said El Gabriel so seriously that the elves didn't say anything back so as not to offend him. They took him by the hand and led him to their parents.

The foundling has been with the elves many times since then and over time he became their friend, but he didn't tell the dwarves.

"El Gabriel," the dwarves repeated.

"Yes," said McOnór, "it has to be El Gabriel, no one else could fulfil the prophecy of the legend now."

But his brother O'Gael made a face of disbelief, for he himself was very experienced in battle and could not imagine that a boy like El Gabriel should be a great warrior, but he dared not contradict the king.

"Bring him here!" They sent for the boy and a little later he stood before the dwarf king for the first time.

"Bring shirt and sword!" the king ordered. They were brought as ordered and the metal shirt was pulled over the human boy's head, reaching down to his knees, as it was made for a great human warrior. El Gabriel didn't know what was happening to him and thought he was going to collapse under the weight of the shirt, but to his surprise he didn't even feel the weight, it was as light as a feather.

"He must learn to fight," murmured the group and the king pressed the sword into his hand. It was also almost weightless. El Gabriel swished it through the air a few times like a willow stick and it hissed. But the dwarves wondered how the boy with the too-long shirt was going to beat the mighty enemy Cal Brighton and his men. Wide-eyed, he heard the legend of his destiny. The boy was not the first to doubt it.

"He needs to concentrate now and get into character," said the king, clapping his hands. In a few minutes, El Gabriel was alone. How had he ended up there? Once again, he let the sword whizz through the air, how he was supposed to beat an army with it was beyond him. As he had so often done recently when seeking advice, he visited the elves in the forest. When he told them what the dwarves expected of him, an old elf said:

"The time has come for you to speak to our queen. You will be travelling for a day, are you ready to leave?"

A few hours later, they were in Cill Aodain. Two female elves led El Gabriel into a large hall made from the trunks of yew trees, their crowns as a ceiling and dense hazel bushes as walls. The carpet was dense forest moss. A vial-like glass vessel protruded from above, emitting a strange light. After a few minutes, the bushes on the far wall parted to form a gateway, through which walked a youthful woman as beautiful as El Gabriel had ever seen in his life. He gazed spellbound at the fairy queen. She appeared to be barely older than El Gabriel. A fluorescent glow emanated from her body and her robe was made of the most beautiful elven silk. When she reached him, she smiled in a way that made the blood rush to his face. She took the boy's hands and he felt a warm power flow through his body.

"So it's you," she said, "we've been expecting you for so long, so much depends on you. The barbarians of Cal Brighton have invaded our sacred land and are threatening to destroy it and enslave its inhabitants. We have certain news that Cal Brighton will advance against Coillte Maghach in the next few days. We elves are not allowed to fight the humans directly and so far that has not been a problem. They don't even know we exist yet, and we've always kept out of human disputes. But now the situation has changed, because the humans have started to destroy our homes. A few days ago, we therefore convened the Great Council of Elves and made the following decisions:

In view of the new facts, we must cease our neutrality and take a stand; we are forbidden to intervene directly in the fighting. We will therefore exert our influence indirectly by endowing you with gifts that are not normally available to humans. But you could do nothing with all this if you did not possess the most important gift yourself: You have learnt - or rather, you have not forgotten - to listen to your heart, because the powers with which we endow you can only be accessed and used through your heart.

Firstly, your protective shirt and sword. The dwarves are excellent miners and craftsmen. They have thus succeeded in making you this extraordinary equipment from Anhánicum. No weapon will penetrate your armoured shirt and your sword will cut through other swords like butter. But that alone is not enough. We give the shirt the power to reflect all the evil that the enemy puts into a blow against the wearer. The shirt will retain this power as long as the user feels no resentment towards the attacker. Thus, the attacker becomes the attacked. We give your sword the power not to kill. Rather, it should turn the enemies it strikes into the swordsman's allies, as long as he does not turn it against them in hatred, but only uses it in his defence. So you will not be able to defeat your enemies with your weapons, but only with your heart. That is why you are the chosen one, El Gabriel, "the great warrior of the heart."

After these words, she placed her hands on her shirt and sword. In a light voice, she spoke words in a language that El Gabriel did not understand. He felt a warm wave flow through his body.

She took the boy's head in both hands and kissed him on the mouth. Liquid gold flowed from there directly into his heart.

"It's love," she whispered in his ear, "only love."

After these words, Al'Dorin disappeared through the hazelnut portal.

El Gabriel sat dazed in the soft moss of the elven queen's reception hall, his head buzzing, his stomach filled with butterflies. He would never forget his encounter with Al'Dorin, her beauty, her words, her love, his love. Slowly he rose, strengthened, ready for the great battle against the tyrant Cal Brighton.

The elf children accompanied him back to Coillte Maghach to the edge of the forest. He floated back to Coillte Anhán, his heart filled with love for Al'Dorin. No sooner had the news of his return spread than McOnór had him summoned to him.

"It is time," he began to speak, "for you to be trained in the use of your sword. My brother O'Gael is our greatest warrior, he is already waiting for you in the armoury to teach you. El

Gabriel said:

"There won't be much opportunity for that, because the Agil Sachá will be attacking in the next few days."

He reported what he had learnt from the elves, but did not mention the encounter with Al'Dorin because he knew that the king did not like her. It was enough that El Gabriel was in their forest, for McOnór's face swelled red and all of Coillte Anhán feared his wrath.

"No dwarf has any business in the forest of elves," he shouted and ran around in circles excitedly.

"You can't trust them, they're evil, devious and sneaky, they're not our friends."

El Gabriel was not impressed by the king. He let him rage a little longer, but his anger quickly subsided. Then he replied:

"I'm not a dwarf, you said so yourself, so I'm not going to behave like one on principle. Besides, the elves are not your enemies, even if they are not friends, they are on our side in this war, that alone should be enough to correspond with them. In times like these, you can't have enough allies. But the most important thing is: if I am to be your hero, as you say, then I must be allowed to choose my friends and comrades. I love you dwarves because you are my home, but the elves have been my friends for a long time because they are exactly the opposite of what is said of them here in Coillte Anhán. They are good, open and honest. So your opinion of them must be wrong and can only stem from the fact that you have never met them."

The king was as astonished by these words as El Gabriel himself, hardly able to believe that it was he who had spoken them. The king looked at the boy for a long time and did not say a word. His face remained white like that of an ordinary dwarf, so an outburst of anger was not to be expected. Rather, it seemed as if he was thinking deeply, and that was exactly what happened.

McOnór tried to remember what exactly the legend said, then he remembered the words:

The legend

When the enemy's hand has already seized

with great power Coillte Anhán,

the bravest cannot win,

The cunningest who know no cunning,

the small people are threatened with extinction

A hero is born out of the greatest of adversities.

A human warrior strong and fine

will be the mediator of his peoples.

With a pure heart and great courage

he leads them into the embers of the enemy,

suffocates the fire, barely ignited,

the enemy's superiority melts away.

Evil recedes, the shadow falls,

the old world is being changed.

Generations will still be singing,

of victory, won in the night,

but not the sword will force it,

fame brings greater power.

What is true today will soon not be true,

a new spirit is emerging in the country,

brings friendship to the people of Anhán,

gave birth to victory, a pure heart.

After a while, the king broke his silence. To El Gabriel's surprise, he said:

"I think I understand now. You are right, my boy: you are the chosen one. Go to O'Gael now, even if we don't have much time left, you can't go into battle completely unprepared. I, for one, will probably have a lot to learn in the near future."

The boy left the king alone and made his way to the armoury. When he entered, O'Gael was already there and had put on his armour, he seemed to have been waiting. He looked unkindly at the boy and grumbled at him in the same way.

"There you are, chosen greenhorn, supposed saviour of our people. Let's see how you will protect us, our king and his people believe in you."

"I'm sorry," El Gabriel replied, "but I didn't choose this role and, like you, I was fulfilling our king's wish. Let's make the best of it. I hope that when we drive out the invaders, you will be with me as an experienced warrior and not leave the greenhorn completely defenceless against his enemies. We don't want to disappoint our king."

Again the boy is surprised at his words, but he

has the feeling that he understands the king's brother, he respects him very much.

O'Gael didn't quite want to go into it, but couldn't continue in the same way.

"Let's get started," he grumbled," you can leave your shirt on, then I can't hurt you and we can fight hard, like it's really going to be. But your sword could be dangerous to me, because whatever I use as a weapon will be destroyed like butter by your sword. If I were the chosen one, with your weapon it would be easy for me to defeat the enemy. But without your tools, there would be no incentive for me to fight with you, so go on, defend yourself as best you can."

With these words, he slashed powerfully at El Gabriel with his sword. In the next moment, he flew across the room as if hit by an invisible fist; he didn't know what hit him. Stunned, he picked himself up.

"I'm sorry," said El Gabriel.

"I didn't even see you hit me, who taught you that?"

Clutching his sword, he crept towards El Gabriel.

"I'll have to be careful after all," he said. The greenhorn wouldn't take him by surprise again.

This time he wanted to take him by surprise. He was a pretty clever fighter and the greenhorn wouldn't see his thrust. He struck without an approach. When he got up this time, he was completely dazed. He looked angrily at the boy.

"You sneaky bastard," he shouted and rushed towards El Gabriel with his sword raised. He had to show the greenhorn. The boy reflexively parried with his sword as O'Gael's hand swung down. The sharp blade of the anhanicum sword pierced the dwarf's forearm; the blade fell from his hand. He looked at his arm, it was unharmed. He held out his hand to the boy and said:

"You can count on me, El Gabriel, I will follow you, faithful to the death, I hereby take this oath."

The boy knew that this was the first victory he had won with the sword. It had been his intention to get the pugnacious O'Gael on his side. It seemed as if the sword was fulfilling his wishes.

"I will have to rely on your loyalty very soon," he said to O'Gael, "I expect an attack from the Cal Brighton hordes in the next few days, I will be in dire need of you and your warriors, I don't know what I would do without your friendship."

He hugged the dwarf and patted him on the shoulder. The next morning around four, O'Gael knocked on his door and called out without waiting:

"Young sir, the Agil Sacha have set up camp about two miles from Coillte Maghach and cut down trees during the night. They seem to be gathering there and are expected to attack later today.

Ten minutes later, El Gabriel was in the King's audience chamber; O'Gael and his officers were already there.

"The time has come, El Gabriel, just as you predicted. An elf informed the guards at the portal to Coillte Anhán in the early hours of the morning. It was the first time in many generations that an elf has made direct contact with a dwarf. Times do indeed seem to be changing, just as the legend says. I ask you to take command of our warriors with immediate effect."

The boy turned to O'Gael:
"Have your officers take the oath of allegiance."

Without hesitation, O'Gael laid his sword at El Gabriel's feet and repeated his oath of allegiance from the previous day, and his officers did the same. It was quickly agreed that they would not wait for the Agil Sacha to attack. The officers explained that the warriors had already been put on alert and would be ready to leave in less than an hour.

Shortly before dawn, they reached the intruders' camp, who seemed to feel safe as only a few guards had been posted. They had no chance of resisting when they were taken by surprise. The camp was already bustling with activity and it seemed as if they were about to leave. Suddenly, a giant of a man with a shock of red hair and a beard that reached down to his chest stepped out of the thicket. The little warriors' sword sheaths rattled in quick succession, but the man raised his hands placatingly:

"Slán, my friends, I am Seán O'Brien of Castlebar and I am here with nine hundred men to attack the Agil Sacha camp. We have been living here in the forests of Coillte Maghach for several months and have been waiting for the day of retribution ever since. But the invaders are heavily outnumbered, a young, handsome man with golden hair informed us shortly after midnight, he spoke of eight thousand men. We alone could not possibly have taken them on, but the handsome youth has already announced your arrival. You should have about two thousand warriors, so that together we will have just under three thousand men. The numerical superiority of the enemy is still overwhelming, so we are considering whether we should dare to attack. I would like to discuss this with your commander, who is he by the way?

The officers of the dwarves pointed to the boy and said in chorus:

"We have sworn allegiance to El Gabriel and we will follow him to the death." Seán O'Brien looked at the boy, obviously taken aback, "but he's still almost a child," he said.

But unimpressed by the giant's words, the boy replied:

"Didn't the elf tell you that the dwarves are led by a young warrior?"

"Yes," replied the redhead, "but I didn't think he would be so young. How many battles have you fought?"

"None yet," El Gabriel replied without embarrassment," and I have no intention of ever beating another one after our victory. As for us, I have no need for consultation, we will definitely attack in a few minutes so that the element of surprise remains on our side, you can decide whether you want to fight with us or prefer to stay out of it, we will accept either decision."

Impressed by the boy's self-confident demeanour, Seán seemed to have forgotten his objection and returned it indignantly:

"Of course we will fight on your side, my men will also follow me, to the death if necessary. We are also ready to attack and see no need to hesitate any longer."

In the meantime, the dwarves had completely surrounded the camp.

"Here we go," the boy said, "we'll form the main front while the warriors scattered around the camp tighten the ring. Are you in our front line?" he asked, addressing O'Brien.

"I'd love to," he replied, "as far forward as possible."

A few minutes later, about twelve hundred men, El Gabriel, Seán O'Brien and O'Gael in the lead, stormed into the camp. Another eighteen hundred rushed in from all sides with loud battle cries. The enemies were frozen in shock for a few seconds; they had not yet taken up arms. There was great confusion in the camp, and many had not yet reached the armoury when they were slain. El Gabriel knew that his hand would not kill, and he was very glad of that, because the enemy also had women and children at home, and most of them had been forced to take up arms. The sooner this fight was over, the fewer of them would die. With lightning speed, he let his sword circle and everyone who was even touched by the blade turned his sword against his comrades. As a result, the number of fighters on El Gabriel's side grew. Those of the enemy who struck at him fell to the ground badly injured or fatally wounded, barely realising what was happening to them. El Gabriel tried as best he could to fend off the attacks because he wanted to spare his opponents a surprise death. His comrades saw him fighting like a lion and his opponents either sinking into the dust or taking his side immediately after their attack. Many of Cal Brighton's soldiers seized the opportunity and followed their examples, even though they had not been hit by El Gabriel's sword. O'Brien's men and the dwarves were caught up in the boy's spirit and became insurmountable for their opponents. Then the unbelievable happened: Cal Brighton suddenly found himself face to face with the boy. He looked grimly at El Gabriel, murderous lust flashing from his eyes. A fight to the death began, whereby, curiously enough, both were only fighting for one life, Cal Brighton's. El Gabriel wanted to spare his opponent at all costs, so he had to avoid being hit by him. If he managed to defeat him, the battle would be over - he knew that. If any of his comrades wanted to rush to his aid, he ordered them to stand back. Brighton was an experienced fighter, so El Gabriel missed him with his sword when he struck at him. Conversely, the boy managed to dodge the Agil Sacha leader's blows. The two stood opposite each other and stared each other down. Then Brighton raised his sword in a flash, only to let the blade whizz down in the next moment. The boy reacted quickly and severed his opponent's blade from the shaft with his Anhánicum sword as if the steel were a mass of bananas. Cal Brighton looked in amazement at the remnant he held in his hand. El Gabriel took advantage of this moment of surprise and plunged the blade into his opponent's chest. Cal Brighton looked him in the eyes, which had lost all expression of murderous lust. The boy pulled the blade from his chest. One of the Agil Sacha officers rushed to his commander. As he raised his sword against El Gabriel, Brighton stopped him with the words:

"Let go, give me your sword."

The officer believed that he wanted to do the job himself and handed him his sword with a smug grin. El Gabriel stood quietly by and waited. The fighting had stopped and all eyes were on the two of them.

As soon as the commander had received the sword, he knelt before El Gabriel and laid the sword at his feet.

"I hereby swear to serve you faithfully with my men and will follow you to my death if ordered to do so."

"That won't be necessary," the boy replied, "I'm just giving you an order: Release the occupied territories of Erin and return to your land in peace. Let your warriors return to their families."

"As you command, Lord, but if you should call me one day, I will hurry to you and fight by your side."

"So be it," said the young hero, "and now go in peace."

Many eyes saw the legend of Anhán come true. The battle went down in legend as the miracle of Coillte Anhán. Just a week later, Cal Brighton had released all of Erin's conquered territories and returned to his homeland with most of his people. Many, however, had befriended the inhabitants and made Erin their home. The story of the miracle of Anhán ends here, but there is one more thing to say. The beautiful Al'Dorin has given up her immortality and become El Gabriel's wife. That is the real miracle. Al'Dorin chose mortality out of love, and this sacrifice will live on in legends long after the miracle of Coillte Anhán has been forgotten".

* * *

When Seán finishes, he and Saóirse look deep into each other's eyes, tears streaming down their cheeks. They have forgotten the world around them and are oblivious to the bard singing Countries in a croaky voice. Then Saóirse breaks the silence:

"That's a wonderful story and I'm deeply impressed. Now people here can say what they like about you. Whatever you've done, it can't really be anything bad. Anyone who tells a story like that with so much feeling must be basically good."

Seán smiles sheepishly:

"Thank you for so much advance confidence, but don't you want to hear what they say about me first?"

"Not today," replies Saóirse, "I want to savour the magic of your story a little longer." She smiles as she adds:

"You can come back to your sins tomorrow if you want, but you really don't owe me an account."

"I want to come back to this, and I think you have a right to, because I've fallen in love with you and I want my lover to know everything about me."

As he says these words, she feels the rumbling in her stomach stronger than it already was.

"I don't know what love feels like yet," she replies, "but if that's what I feel, I don't think there's any doubt that I've fallen in love too."

Seán holds her hand tightly in his and looks at her. The next few minutes need no words, the eyes tell everything. The world around them doesn't seem to exist.

The entertainer has finished his 'Whisky in the Jar'. Such well-known Dublin classics await many tourists now visiting the island during the holiday season. Promisingly, the singer announces 'Wild Rover', the last song he can get away with before the obligatory 'Sinne Fianna Fáil'. As he begins, he snaps the lovers out of their reverie; there are worse reasons to leave.

It's half past eleven (half past eleven on the continent) when they arrive on Market Street, too early to end the evening. The 'no-never-never' from the pub no longer reaches here, but the hustle and bustle in the town is at its peak. It's hardly quieter here than in the pub. Seán has wrapped both arms around Saóirse, she has her arms around his waist and Saóirse has the first kiss of her life. The noisy night people of the city do not exist. They are not two and not one, not singers and not music, not dancers and dance, they are a universe.

Now Saóirse knows, no, she doesn't just know, she experiences what love is. She has lived like the frog that sits in the meadow next to the most beautiful flowers and yet doesn't know what honey tastes like. Now she is a bee and tastes the sweet flavour of love. After a small eternity, time begins again for her, the spaceship returns, but the feeling of infinity remains as her lips part.

"I love you," she breathes and no longer has to think, it feels right.

"Do you have to go back tonight?" Seán asks quietly, as if he doesn't want to break the spell that surrounds her.

"For nothing in the world," she whispers.

"I only have a small flat, you know that I actually live in Dublin."

"A lily pad would be big enough for us," she breathes.

"Or a meadow," says Seán, "a meadow as a bed, a roof of stars and music from Maestro Nature's orchestra."

"I know where this inn is," says Saóirse, her voice still muffled.
"The bed is soft and fragrant, the roof is studded with millions of diamonds, a great master conducts the concert of soloists, marvellous musicians like the river, the wind and the animals."

"Yes," says Seán, "that's where we want to spend the night."

"It's twenty minutes down to Glore," she says, "let's just take a blanket with us because it can get quite chilly there at night, even in summer."

"I have sleeping bags at home, so we should be warm enough."

"Then let's not waste any time."
A shiver of joy runs through her body; spending the night alone with her lover in one of her favourite places means the greatest happiness for her at this moment.

A short time later, they are on the path, passing Cultrasna and Corrib and the last cottage, after which they descend steeply to the river. They walk the last few metres to the bridge, laughing and having fun. He exuberantly throws the sleeping bags over the stone wall at the end of the bridge and jumps over in one leap. He gallantly offers her his hand.

Although she had climbed over here alone several times before, she gladly accepts his help. She lets herself fall trustingly into his arms from the wall, he holds her tightly and kisses her, her lips open willingly. They stroll hand in hand along the river, which roars to their left, confirming his presence.

"Let's stay here," she says, as tall grass promises a cosy place to lie down. He unrolls the sleeping bags and spreads them out on the ground.

"Let's sit and listen for a while," he says quietly. They sink into the soft fabric and gaze into the rushing glow, close together, cheek to cheek. No words are necessary, because they both feel the same. There is almost no wind, the gentle fanning of the air is drowned out by the sound of the river. The night is clear and the panorama of stars interweaves it with infinity. If there is a supreme happiness, it is what they both feel now.

"I can combine the sleeping bags into one big one," he says after a while, "or would you like your own?"

"Make it a big one," she replies. Minutes later, they are lying snuggled up close to each other. Although they are fully clothed, she can feel his arousal. Saóirse knows what it is; Old Méabh had told her early on. But it is different to hear about it and to feel it. She remembers what Old Méabh told her about love. Yes, that is what she wants, closely united with her beloved.

"Shall we do it?" she whispers.

"There's nothing I want more," he replies and she senses his arousal more strongly. "But I'm not allowed to, not now," he continues.

"What's stopping you?" she asks Seán.

"The unspoken," he says, "I can't do it until you know me, and I can't do it for any other reason."

Saóirse is a little disappointed, if she can't find out with Seán, who can she find out with? But she tells herself that Seán will have good reasons.

"Let it go," she says, "we'll talk tomorrow and you'll tell me what bad thing you've done. But let's not think about it now, the night is too beautiful."

She snuggles up close to him and savours the effect. They lie there for a long time and surrender again and again in fierce kisses until sleep envelops them.

It is already bright morning when a giant tractor thundering over the bridge wakes them from their sleep. They are still lying entwined and look at each other in surprise. They only slowly realise where they are.

"Good morning, my love," he says with a laugh as she opens her eyes, "how did you sleep in our hostel?"

She lolls and answers:

"Fantastic, the best bed in the world. But now I'm ravenous."

"Good," he says, "I'll invite you to my place for breakfast, we just need to get toast, hash browns, eggs and sausages." "And coffee," she says, "and milk," he adds.

"Isn't it easier to go to the breakfast café?" asks Saóirse.

"You're right, much easier," he says, "besides, it's chaos at home, too much so to receive my beloved properly."

In Mary's coffee shop, they hold their coffee cups with both hands and look at each other wordlessly. Formless thoughts buzz around in their heads, the echo of a magical night. Mary serves herself, a rich Irish breakfast with a smiling "Lovely Day."

"Beautiful," comes the reply from their lips at the same time, and they dreamily return Mary's smile.

They eat their breakfast with a good appetite, Seán helps a little and together they don't leave any leftovers.

Diamond Valley

"Let's do something," says Seán, "I've got a car here in the village and the weather is very nice. Maybe we'll go to Enniscrone. We'll be alone on the Atlantic and I can talk to you there. Do you know the beautiful beach in Killala Bay?"

"It's been a long time since I was there with my parents and siblings, I think I was too little to remember.

"All the better," he replies, "in this sunshine today you can see the 'diamonds' glittering on the beach; maybe you still remember 'Diamond Valley' after all."

"I know it's called that because it's so sparkly. I still have time today, I'd love to go there with you," says Saóirse.

"We'll be there in an hour," says Seán, "we shouldn't waste any time."

They get up and he pays for breakfast. A few minutes later, Seán's old Volvo is already rolling along Bohola Road. Later, they pass Foxford and Ballina and drive along the banks of the River Moy towards Enniscrone.

Saóirse senses a building tension and she knows that something wants to come out of him, she thinks about how she could help him.

"I don't have a good reputation in Kiltimagh," Seán begins.

"We've been this far before," Saóirse replies with a smile, and then she has an idea of how to make it easier for him. So she continues:

"People have prejudices, I've experienced that first-hand. I haven't told you and the others everything about myself either. People are also prejudiced against people like me."

Seán looks at her, shaking his head.

"What prejudices should anyone have against you? In my case, the reputation is even partly justified, at least if you don't know the background."

"It's the same with me," Saóirse insists, "I also have a reputation, or rather, not just me, but all my people."

Seán seems to have forgotten what he was going to say, he seems amused.

"Are you a criminal family?" he asks jokingly, but Saóirse doesn't laugh.

"Many will see it that way," she says. She notices Seán's confusion and he is surprised at the seriousness with which she has said this. She continues: "I'm what most people call a Tinker, but we call ourselves Pavee or Traveller."

At this moment, she realises how good it feels to stand by her own origins.

"You?", he says, "you don't look like that at all."

"Do you see? You have prejudices too, what must we look like?"

"You're right," replies Seán meekly, "that was a stupid remark."

"She wasn't that stupid," she replies, "what can you say if you only know us by sight. You've probably grown up with the stories that are told about us and sometimes they're even true. The fact is that we also have good and bad. People tend to see what they want to see. In our case, they have chosen to see the bad. We are people from whom the 'decent' have to protect themselves. Many years ago, I myself experienced how business people closed their shops when I came to the city with my brothers. So as a member of a Traveller family, I also have a bad reputation, whether I'm good or bad."

"I know your reputation," says Seán, "but you're not personally responsible for it, like I am for mine. I mean, you don't have a bad reputation of your own. Besides, I don't care if you're a Traveller or not, you're the girl I love, everything else is secondary."

"You see," she replied, "my feelings for you won't change if you tell me about your misdeeds - unless it's something really bad, but I rule that out with you. But look, I think we've reached our destination."

They are actually driving into Enniscrone, with the inviting white beach to the left. Seán steers the car through a kind of driveway, and then the white, glittering splendour lies before them. He drives a long way along the beach between the water and the dunes, almost as far as where the Moy flows into the Atlantic. Despite the glorious weather, the beach down here is deserted. He takes a left turn towards the dunes and stops.

"Let's walk along the beach for a while," he says, "then it'll be easier for me."

They take off their shoes and socks and pull up their trouser legs. Holding hands, they wade through the water so that the crashing waves slap against their calves. The sound of the sea and wind penetrates deep into them. No words are spoken for a long time, they are too caught up in this atmosphere. They don't realise how long they have been walking when he gently pulls them towards the dunes. Here, a narrow, glistening path leads up the sandy hill.

"It really does look like a path interspersed with diamonds," Saóirse breaks the sacred silence.

"Yes," he says absent-mindedly, "this is the right place." He gently pulls Saóirse down to him in the sand. The sound of the sea seems far away and even the wind has lost its power; it is quiet all around.

"I'm not allowed to love you," he begins abruptly, "and yet I can't help it." She takes his hand and squeezes it. Whatever he says, she is determined not to interrupt him.

"It's true," he continues, "that I'm partly responsible for my reputation, even if it's none of people's business. I've had the odd affair, not in Kiltimagh, but in Balla and Swinford. But it doesn't matter, word gets around very quickly here, even beyond the city limits, especially in my status."

He pauses, as if he needs to clarify his status. Saóirse doesn't interrupt him, although she notices his agony, she waits patiently. He sits there for a long time and says nothing, he seems far, far away. Saóirse remains silent.

Then he suddenly says:

"I have a wife and two children in Dublin."

Saóirse feels the ground being pulled out from under her feet. She feels weak, something clenches around her heart, but she remains silent.

"I love my wife," he continues, "and especially my children. The people in Kiltimagh know about them, I haven't told them, but the wind has carried it over. So far it's been okay, the affairs were not a contradiction for me, they meant nothing to me. You should know that the sexual relationship between my wife and I has diminished considerably in recent years, in other words, there's not much going on between us in this relationship. I don't know why that is, I used to think that the desire would never change. Maybe it's just us, I don't know how it is with others. Despite everything, it doesn't change anything about my feelings for my wife.

However, the reputation as such has its own particular issues. Some women in the village despise or even hate me because they see themselves in the role of the betrayed. The men are more relaxed about it, but let's leave that alone, it's not important here.

My dilemma began with you. I didn't expect something like this to happen, but I fell in love with you. No, I fell in love with you and I really love you now. But when I think about my wife, my love for her hasn't diminished. I have found myself in a hopeless situation. I want nothing more than to live the rest of my life with you, but I also want that with my wife and even more so with my children. But at the same time, I know it's impossible. What am I supposed to do? Can you empathise with my drama?"

Saóirse is still holding his hand, only tighter than before. She feels a pain she had never felt before. She had believed that nothing could shake her, whatever Seán told her. Now she sits, deeply affected, feeling hatred rising within her towards the unknown woman, or is it what the Old Méabh calls jealousy? She feels that this hatred is wrong. Oh, if only Old Méabh were here, she had never needed her more than at this moment. She thinks about what the old woman would advise her here. She remembers, she had already told her:

Listen to your heart! '

But her heart is a mixture of pain, hatred and despair. The call of the heart is silent, the old woman had told Méabh.

Seán has been silent for a long time, he doesn't dare look at her. She puts her hand on his cheek and turns his head towards her, forcing him to look at her.

"My poor darling!" she says, "I don't want to be in your place. I know all about you now, whatever happens now, there's nothing wrong. Come on, let's make love, here and now, but you have to help me. It's the first time for me."

Surprised, he looks at her and says:

"But after everything I've told you?"

She puts her index finger to his lips.

"That's not important here at this moment, make me your wife."

She reaches her hand under his T-shirt and gently runs it over his stomach and chest. Slowly, his hands rise to embrace her, to caress and fondle her. Then Saóirse becomes his wife. They lie in the warm sand of the dunes for a long time afterwards, embraced tightly.

"Now you're my husband," she says. "Yes," he says.

"I am releasing you now," she continues, "you will return to your wife and children. We will both remain husband and wife, but you will live with your family. Talk to your wife, one must never stop talking. You have a place in my heart for all time, no one will displace you there. But when we are back in Kiltimagh, we will part ways. I will not return to Kiltimagh. Whatever I was looking for, I have found it. Maybe I'll be lucky and carry a child of yours under my heart."

She gently releases herself from his embrace.

"Come on, my love, let's go back."

Seán was in a daze, but now he protests:

"But you can't be serious, we can't separate, we have to stay together, I love you."

"I know," she replies, "I love you too, more than anyone else in this world, but we only have a chance to keep our love if we separate. I have to give you up because I love you, there's no other way. Let's not make it any harder, I will suffer, suffer endlessly. I know it won't be any easier for you." She holds out her hand to him. "Let's go back."

Seán rises apathetically and they walk back to the car. He pulls her close once more and they kiss passionately. On the way, he clutches the steering wheel tightly.

"We'll find a way," he says, "it's all better than breaking up, we'll stay together, you'll see."

"Of course, my beloved", but Saóirse understands it differently from him. When they arrive in Kiltimagh, Saóirse still has a few hours before her father picks her up at the church.

"Let's use the few hours we have left so that you can learn about me and my people, you shall know the person you will love for the rest of your life."

Saóirse was sure that Seán loved her as much as she loved him, convinced that the separation would preserve this love forever. She knows that he doesn't believe in this separation at this moment, she lets him have the illusion.

In Joyce's Bar, she tells him about the life of the Pavee, about her parents and above all about the Old Méabh. She talks about the prejudices people have against her people. She encourages him to contradict these prejudices wherever he encounters them. Contradicting the errors of the majority takes courage. She knows that he has this courage. Time passes quickly and Seán wants to hold on to her when the hour has come. Saóirse stands up, leans down and kisses him passionately.

"Farewell, my beloved, you have made me your wife, but I cannot live with you. God bless and protect your wife, your children and you."

He tries to hold her by the arm, but she breaks away and leaves the pub without turning round again. Crying loudly, she walks through the night, not bothered that people turn to look at her. Her father's car is already parked at the church, but as she approaches, she realises that he is not alone.

Saóirse rushes towards the car in a panic, tears open the back door and throws herself into Méabh's arms, crying:

"Oh Méabh, I didn't realise how painful it can be when you listen to your heart."

Dream glider (poetry)

I have left the ship,
drifting between rocks of consciousness towards an unknown shore.
 My own self is waiting there.
I still don't know how I should meet it;
whether it wants to surrender to the drifting in the dream sea of vanity,
the gliding in the time divergence between being and existence,
the wanderer between the grave of memory and the mystery of the future,
the longing, the call for knowledge
and the love of the self.
Dazed, I cling to the driftwood of primal consciousness,
surrendering to the whispering dream figures which flatter the pleading I AM.

Time travel to Knockcroghery

The journey is very strenuous. He has rarely travelled the tour from Germany via Calais-Dover up to Holyhead in one day. This time he had to be in Galway the very next morning. He had a three-and-a-half-hour rest on the ferry to Dublin, but now he was already turning onto the national road that would take him westwards. At this time of year, it is already dark for a long time and the misty rain is not helping to make the journey any easier. The stretch of motorway behind Dublin is still passable, but then the road becomes single-lane and narrow. There's not much traffic heading west on this Saturday after Christmas. He passes Enfield, a welcome change with its brightly lit shops and pubs. Now he has the lights of the town behind him.

He should have got a room there, because now, on the dark streets in this rainy atmosphere, he is overcome by tiredness. He has to turn into a country lane and stop because he is in danger of falling asleep. But the tiredness is blown away, he hesitates and decides to drive on.

Now there is a knock on the back window and he is startled. He looks back and recognises a male figure soaked by the rain in the light of the rear headlights. He closes the door from the inside and rolls down the window a little. Now, in the light of the interior lamp, the man does not appear threatening. When asked what he wants, he answers in accent-free German:

"Excuse me, I saw your licence plate and I assume you're German."

He is surprised and relieved to hear the language he is familiar with under these circumstances.

"Which direction are you travelling in from Kinnegad, Longford or Roscommon?"

A short time later, they drive together on the road to Kinnegad and turn off onto the national road to Galway. His companion's name is Michael, here they call him Mike. He moved from Aachen to Knockcroghery forty years ago with his parents, who had bought a small farm. He has lived there ever since and took over the farm after his parents died. He is now the father of three children himself. Back then, thirty years ago, there weren't many settlers in the area. The driver is pretty sure that his companion is Michael, who was his best friend back then.

The journey through time

At the age of fifteen, he spent a year as a guest
on a farm near Lough Ree. The Schmidt family
picked him up from the railway station in
Athlon, everyone had come: His father Josef,
whom he later called Joe, his mother
Annemarie, known as Ann, the ten-year-old
twins Rósín and Aileen and Michael. He was
allowed to sit on the front of the buckboard,
with two lively Irish ponies trotting in front of
them. The children romped around in the back
of the loading area. The twins had a strange
English accent, which he didn't understand at the
time. Every now and then his name came up and
they laughed, which embarrassed him. Ann,
noticing his insecurity, spoke to him to distract
him. He learnt that they were called Smith and
that only German was spoken at home. As soon
as they left the house, they spoke English, Irish
was not common in these parts. Joe held the
reins the whole time and gave the animals
commands. Somewhere after Knockcroghery,
they turned right onto a narrow track and it was
another fifteen minutes or so before they
reached the farm.

In the glow of a small village, he now looks at
Michael, called Mike, from the side and recognises
him with certainty. Mike, for his part, shows not a

hint of a clue, but he doesn't dare touch the old wound.

At that time, there were still two weeks to go before the course started, so he had enough time to get to know the family beforehand. The farmers' work was not as commonplace as it was on German farms. The work on the farm was limited to sheep and cattle breeding. Nobody got up before eight o'clock in the morning. Ann was usually the first one up, and the twins arrived when the sausages, bacon and eggs were cooked. He quickly got used to not arriving for breakfast until around nine, just like Joe and Mike. He still remembers going into town with Joe one evening and having his first pint. At home in Germany, he wasn't allowed to drink beer, but here a boy of fifteen was given a pint for the first time. He still remembers how bitter the black beer tasted, but he didn't let on.

Around half past eight, boys and girls with musical instruments came into the pub for a session, as they say here. He felt transported to a strange world. He often heard this typical music later on. That evening, it was the last thing he remembered.

In the time that followed, he began to explore Lough Ree with Mike. Mike showed him how to steer a boat and how to catch pike. They were together from morning till night, and three times a week they went into town with Joe to a pub, but he had had enough of beer for the time being. Joe said it was the only place to get news. Ann went along on Saturdays because there was dancing in the evening.

The holidays passed quickly and he was introduced to school.

He looks over at Mike, who is talking about the past. He must recognise him at any moment, he says. The companion is talking about the twins, who, curiously enough, are also married to a pair of twins from the neighbouring village.

"I lost my parents at an early age," says Mike. Joe died of a heart attack at the age of 59. Two years later, Ann also died of cancer. Mike pauses briefly in his story, the driver can feel his dismay, which also takes hold of him. He had grown fond of Joe and Ann back then. The familiar feeling of still having so much to say and now having missed the chance once and for all comes over him and he tries to keep his composure on this strange night.

Back then, at home in Germany, he had written little more than a polite letter. He received two more from the family, one of which he barely answered. What had happened had affected him too much and he was glad when it was over. Since then, he had never heard from the Schmidts again.

Mike pulled himself together and now talks about Siobhán.

"She was the prettiest in the county," he enthuses, "a lot of guys wanted her, but I got her," Mike continues.

The driver feels uneasy, touched by his behaviour at the time, but fortunately Mike doesn't seem to suspect anything.

> Four weeks before his stay in Ireland came to an end, they met Siobhán at a dance in the city on a Saturday. He fell head over heels in love with her. She seemed to be interested in him too, and he remembered that it annoyed Mike that she didn't pay attention to him. Whispering conspiratorially, Mike reminded him of the vow he had made at the lake that nothing and no one was to come between them. The guest boy pretended to respect this that evening, but secretly arranged to meet Siobhán the following Sunday. Over the next few days, Mike seemed strange and awkward to him. That didn't bother him, because he was in love.
>
> That Sunday evening, the beginning of his first date, was like a dream, his first kiss with a girl.

But around midnight, Mike turned up and sat down at their table as a matter of course. Contrary to his expectations, he was friendly, even though he was slightly drunk. He was happy for him, the most beautiful girl in town for his best friend. Mike stared blatantly into Siobhán's eyes. His subsequent intimate compliments annoyed the guest boy. But her receptiveness made him angry. He had learnt back then that jealousy doesn't look particularly sexy on girls. As he was not yet ready for this lesson, he let things escalate, in short: he messed everything up. He lost Siobhán to Mike, at least that was his stupid view of things. He blamed Mike and became his enemy.

He could hardly bear the fortnight's holiday until his return to Germany and spent it alone with his pain on the shores of Lough Ree. Somehow he managed to say goodbye to the Smith family.

In the next headlights of an oncoming car, the driver sees Mike's stricken face.

"Siobhán died in a car accident ten years ago," he says, "she lived and worked in Dublin. As she was driving to work in the morning, her car skidded during an overtaking manoeuvre and crashed. She ended the relationship with me when she moved to Dublin to study. I really loved her, but I couldn't keep her."

The driver is just as affected, it's as if he really had
just lost her. Maybe everything would have turned
out differently if he hadn't behaved so stupidly back
then. Who knows, if he had apologised. But he was
a stupid boy. His thoughts revolved around 'what
if'. He almost forgets that he is not alone.

"It was a big deal back here in the city," Mike
continued, pulling the driver out of his thoughts.

"It took the love of my life away from me and I still
haven't got over it. Who knows, maybe we would
have got back together after her return."

Mike has no idea that his driver's wound is more
recent.

"Excuse me," Mike continues, "sometimes
memories come back to life. We've arrived, you
can let me off here.

We have actually arrived in Knockcroghery. Mike
thanks him profusely and suggests we visit him
soon so that he can tell us about himself. He
describes the way to his farm, which he knows so
well.

It's a new day and he's already done his business in
Galway. So he decides to go to Knockcroghery
and make himself known to his old friend. After
sleeping on it, his reticence of the previous night

seems ridiculous. After all, the bad humour of that night had been a youthful folly that he had actually overcome in life. But in his tense state last night, he has reverted to the mood of his youth. The memory now seems surreal to him, and it's time he met his old friend Mike as a man.

***

He is confused. Back in Knockcroghery, he finds the ruins of the familiar house instead of the farmhouse. He has to go to the village, because in Ireland the safest place to get information is in the pubs. He learns from an old farmer that Mike died of leukaemia about four years after his stay. Siobhán had married a landlord from Moate. A year after Mike's death, the family returned to Germany. Since then, the old farmhouse has been empty. Behind closed doors, the old man whispers to him:

" The farmhouse is haunted and nobody likes to stay there after dark..."

***

The Storyteller of Tralee

Long before televisions took over living rooms and pubs (social media was still far in the future), storytellers in Ireland entertained people from time to time. In the villages, people would gather in the pub lounges by the fireside to listen to the storytellers' tales. It was not uncommon for a good storyteller's tale to go on for several days. On the days in question, people would eagerly await the evening that would bring the continuation of a story. Ale and stout flowed freely and with every pint the scary story became scarier, the mysterious one more mysterious and the funny one funnier. It was usually older, experienced women or men who had the best stories to tell, and nobody knew whether they had made them up or experienced them.

Following on from those times, the so-called Storyteller Festivals are held in many places every year. The country's storytellers gather to revive the old Irish tradition for a few days. People in villages and towns forget their television sets or other time-killers and come together, just like in the old days.

During a festival in Kiltimagh, I was sitting in Joyce's Bar when an expected storyteller from Tralee, County Clare, entered the dining room. It was still the humble Joyce's, with the small bar, and

Visasvis, as if abandoned by American emigrants, the relic of a corner shop with a counter, a museum of old boxes and tins. It was Joyce's as it was known in Anny Joe's time, the time when the old lady with the girlish smile was still the landlady there.

The artist was well known here, and when he was greeted with applause, I knew it was him too. People immediately gathered in a circle around him, who had taken a seat on a raised chair. I have forgotten his name, but the story he had to tell is all the more vivid in my memory:

"You know me as a storyteller who has never run out of material for a story. You may also know that I only tell what I have really experienced myself or what I have been told by trusted sources whose veracity I would never doubt. And yet, even those who know me will not believe what happened to me many years ago."

When you have no more stories.

I was still quite a young man when I had already gained local fame as a storyteller. Young and old, many much older than me, gathered every evening in our village pub to hear my stories. I don't think I'm exaggerating when I say that I was already a master storyteller. Then it happened:

It was St Patrick's Day when, out of the blue, it occurred to me that everyone now knew all my stories and I had nothing left to tell. On that day of all days, everyone expected something exciting or funny from me. As I didn't feel up to this pressure of expectation, I packed up what I needed and left my home village like an exile to escape the expected disgrace.

I had travelled many roads since then and had hired myself out as a day labourer in several places, but I had never tried to support myself again with the help of my art. One day I also came to Kiltimagh. Nobody knew me here then. It was late when I arrived and the pubs had already closed. Only here in Joyce's did I still hear voices. I knocked on the door, cautiously at first, then forcefully and finally brazenly, I needed a place to stay for the night. Finally, an old lady opened the door, took one quick look at me and suddenly pulled me into the pub by the wrist.

The place was still buzzing, the small room was packed and countless voices were buzzing around the room. I had a few pints and was in a very good mood when I realised that all the guests had left except me. The old lady stood next to me and said:

'I don't know what else you're looking for, but I assume you at least need somewhere to sleep for the night, and I can give you that.

You can imagine how grateful I was for this offer.

The storyteller bowed towards Anny Joe:

"Your mum was a great woman, Ann."

Anny Joe showed her best smile.

"Well," the narrator continued, "the old lady led me up two narrow flights of stairs into a room that I will never forget for the rest of my life. When she switched on a lamp, I saw a large water tank under the ceiling at the opposite end, gurgling loudly. On the right was a couch covered with a lace blanket. An antique cupboard contained ornate pious objects. On a table in the centre of the room, from which the lamp shone, were all sorts of utensils whose use

I couldn't place. She invited me to make myself comfortable on the bed.

When she had gone, I switched off the lamp and lay down immediately. The gurgling, sometimes more, sometimes less, didn't let me fall asleep for a long time. Suddenly I woke up, I must have fallen asleep after all. I felt as if I had heard noises downstairs in the pub. In fact, there was a rumble from downstairs at that moment. I thought someone in the house was still working and turned to my side to go back to sleep, then there was a shrill scream, as if someone feared for their life. I sat upright in bed and turned my attention downwards. Whispering voices were now hurriedly coming up from there. I felt uneasy and tried to find the lamp on the table. It was pitch black in the room, so I had to feel around for it. I was sure I had seen it there, but my hands couldn't feel it. Then a bloodcurdling scream broke through the darkness and I reflexively ducked. My body shook with fear and I tried to think of plausible explanations. But I couldn't even think of a halfway plausible explanation, or maybe I didn't want to know. I heard half-loud mumbling, there must have been at least a dozen men down there.

After spending some time crouched down, I took heart and decided to sneak downstairs and have a careful look. I didn't feel comfortable in my skin, but I managed to sneak up to the door of the pub. There was a strange noise coming from the room that didn't seem to come from human voices, then another death scream that went through me. Cold sweat stood on my forehead. I was unable to escape or enter the pub, I stood there frozen, clutching the door handle. Then a man's voice said:

'There's someone at the door, I can smell it.

I was gripped by cold horror; I had been discovered.

'Shall we invite him round? ' I heard from another voice, 'then he won't have to listen at the door like a thief. '

'Yes, let's bring him to us,' said a third, 'let him tell us why he's spying on us. '

'Hey you,' called another, 'come in and show yourself if you have nothing to hide. '

Although I was paralysed with fear, my body moved mechanically, without my will but also without me being able to stop it, I could no longer escape.

There was a large round table in the middle of the pub, around which twelve fierce male figures were actually sitting. The lamp that I could no longer find upstairs in my bedroom was burning in the centre. I saw no sign of the tormented woman I had assumed was here. One of them pointed to a thirteenth empty chair:

'Just like then, you hid behind the door to avoid your task. Sit down! We've been waiting for you, now we're all here. '

This statement touched me even more strangely than the previous one. I tried not to let my anxiety show and sat down as I was told. The same speaker continued:

'Today marks the seven hundredth anniversary of the day our brother George McOlean was treacherously murdered by his wife Máire. We other thirteen brothers had convicted, sentenced and beheaded this serpent. On this occasion, we come together here every one hundred years to force a confession from the damned Máire. We have just received it. '

Then he turned his face towards me and spoke:

'Brother Jeremiah, you have come at just the right time to execute judgement once again, you know that your hand wields the sword of vengeance. '

A cold sweat ran down my spine, I had fallen in with madmen. A poor woman had been tortured under a ludicrous pretext to force this so-called confession; I could now categorise the death screams. Now I was supposed to kill this unfortunate creature.

'Get the delinquent,' said the speaker to one of his brothers. He rose and disappeared into the back room. A few seconds later, he led in a young woman in a bloodstained white dress, her eyes blindfolded with a black blindfold. She was a very pretty woman, but her face had the agonised expression of a maltreated woman. The 'brother' took the blindfold from her eyes and sat down again. Then the speaker stood up and announced:

'Máire McOlean, you have been convicted of the dastardly murder of your husband. '

At these words, Máire's face darkened and, to my astonishment, I recognised guilt in it.

'That is why we have condemned you to death by beheading. Our brother Jeremiah will carry out this judgement. '

The brothers in the circle nodded and murmured:

'So be it. '

The men got up from their chairs and I did the same. One disappeared into the back room, six others grabbed the young woman and laid her backwards on the table. One of them pushed a large roll under her neck. Meanwhile, the man came back, carrying a long sword. He gripped the sword with both hands above the shaft and handed it to me.

'Take this sword of vengeance, brother Jeremiah, and carry out our judgement. This woman has killed one of your brothers, and you have the enviable task of judging her. '

I grabbed the sword willlessly, but then I couldn't do it anymore.

'You're not my brothers,' I shouted, 'I've never seen you before in my life. '

But the men didn't react, they mumbled in chorus:

'Judge the condemned, Jeremiah, judge her. '

They repeated these words like a prayer wheel, over and over again. I raised the sword as if paralysed, with the poor murderess beneath me, who was staring fearfully at the deadly blade at that moment.

'I can't kill her,' it pounded in my head. Then I shouted out:

'You're crazy, I can't kill her. '

The sword in my hands became heavy, the room swayed, I felt dizzy. The action spun faster and faster.

***

Epilogue

I sat in bed, drenched in sweat, with the landlady next to me with her arm around me.

"Quiet," she said, "you were dreaming. It's not good to dream bad stories, it's better to tell them."

The man from Tralee paused and looked round. Now I remembered that his name was actually Jeremias McOlean. It was dead quiet in the pub; everyone knew that his story wasn't over yet. Then he continued with a mischievous expression:

"The lamp that I had seen on the judging brothers' table that night was still missing from my hostel room. I didn't dare ask about it. But since then, I have been able to tell stories again. If I can't think of anything again, I'll tell the story about a storyteller who couldn't tell any more stories."